enty-Four Vagabond Twenty-

The Spit, the Sound and the Nest

Kathrine Sowerby

Vagabond Voices
Glasgow

© Kathrine Sowerby 2017

First published on 22 May 2017 by
Vagabond Voices Publishing Ltd.,
Glasgow,
Scotland.

ISBN 978-1-908251-79-4

The author's right to be identified as author of this book under the Copyright, Designs and Patents Act 1988 has been asserted.

Printed and bound in Poland

Cover design by Mark Mechan

Typeset by Park Productions

The publisher acknowledges subsidy towards this publication from Creative Scotland

ALBA | CHRUTHACHAIL

For further information on Vagabond Voices, see the website, www.vagabondvoices.co.uk

*A sign read: Nobody, at any time, should allow
themselves to be lifted off their feet*

Contents

The Spit   1

The Sound   55

The Nest   107

The Spit

The bus turned in the widest part of the road and Felix and Luc watched it drive back the way it had come, until the noise of the engine vanished. The night air caught in Felix's throat and he grabbed Luc's sleeve and tugged him closer. Luc tripped over the rucksack at his feet. "I can't see anything," he said, "and it's freezing."

"I'm sure there was a signpost," said Felix. "Where's the lighter?"

"I've got it," said Luc. He rasped his thumb on the ignition a couple of times before the flame jumped up in front of Felix's face.

"Hey," said Felix, "watch my hair."

Felix reached out and found the rough edge of a wooden post. Keeping hold of it, he pulled Luc towards him. "Here," said Felix and he traced his finger over letters carved into the wood. Luc dropped the lighter into the snow and clutched his hand. "What d'you do that for?" said Felix.

"My thumb was burning."

"Let's just sit for a second."

"It's cloudy, that's the problem," said Luc. "But we're here."

They hauled their bags together and sat on them, back to back, listening to the creak and moan of the trees until it was joined by a kind of humming. "Did you hear that?" said Felix. It was getting louder, coming towards them.

"Hello." Luc called out into the night.

"Just a minute," a voice replied.

A beam of light darted left and right, highlighting

the hem of a coat, piles of dirty snow and feet encased in slippers, before shining directly at them. Felix and Luc shielded their eyes. The man lowered the torch and held it at his chest, illuminating their faces.

"Where did you two come from?" he said.

"The bus dropped us here," said Luc.

"Is somebody meeting you?"

Luc shook his head.

"Well, you better follow me then." The man pointed a tunnel of light along the road. "My name's Joseph," he said. Felix looked in Luc's direction but they were bathed in darkness again. He reached out and caught Luc's hand. The light shuffled away.

"We can't just sit here till morning." Felix said. They grabbed their bags, threw them over their shoulders and ran towards the fading light.

Rita pushed back the quilt and climbed out of bed. She stood on the rug listening to Joseph, waiting to hear if there were voices to answer his questions. Her nightgown brushed against her knees as she peeled her cardigan from the back of a chair. His voice grew louder until the bedroom door slammed open. Paint cracked and fell to the floor where the handle hit the wall.

"Rita, you're awake."

She peered past him at the boys, stooped under the weight of their rucksacks. Joseph gestured back to his find. "They were at the bus stop, just arrived," he said. "Lucky I came along when I did."

Felix gave a small wave. Luc stepped forward offering her his hand to shake. Rita gathered her hair from around her shoulders, twisted it and let it fall in a single braid down her spine. "You must be exhausted," she said. "Come and sit down."

Joseph turned sideways to let her pass and Rita glanced down at his feet. It was the middle of the night and Joseph's slippers were soaked through. Again. He took them off and stood them by the stove while Rita poured milk into a saucepan. When it began to froth, she stirred in spoonfuls of cocoa and sugar then carried the mugs to the table, savouring the burn against her knuckles. While the boys drank, she looked around the room in the half-light as if she was seeing it for the first time. Seascapes hung on the wall, she'd tried to make it homely, but the wallpaper was dirty and Joseph's newspapers were spread all over the floor. "We weren't expecting anyone," she said. "Will you be staying long?" Joseph put his hand on Rita's shoulder.

"They can stay as long as they like," he said.

The spare room was bare except for a bookcase and two mattresses slumped against the wall that had been left by the previous owners. A photograph of a sunset hung above a bleached out rectangle where a bed must have been. Felix picked up a bird's nest from the windowsill. He pressed some loose tufts of moss back between the entwined twigs and put it down.

"We don't use this room, really," said Rita.

"It's fine," said Felix. They hadn't thought about where they were going to sleep that night. It had all been about getting away, not about arriving. Now, with sleep in sight he felt grateful for the hospitality.

"Joseph, can you fetch some bedding," said Rita, "we all need to get some rest."

Felix and Luc eased the mattresses on to the floor and laid them side by side. The light from the bulb was harsh. "There's a spare lamp somewhere," said Rita.

Joseph came back with a pile of sheets and blankets and Rita left them making the beds to hunt in the cupboard in her room. Her breath was quick. She pulled the stool from under her dressing table to stand on and at the back, on a stack of shoeboxes, an art deco lamp lay on its side with its flex wound round its base. The boxes were sealed but as she reached for the lamp, she saw one had been opened with a clean cut through the parcel tape. She lifted it down. The box was filled to the brim with loose photos: Joseph before his hair turned white looking into the face of a newborn, a woman in a short skirt cradling a baby wrapped in a long shawl. Her skin was smooth, her lips red. Rita barely recognised herself. She put the lid back on the box and slid it into position, took the lamp and hurried down the hall to where Joseph stood with his finger pressed against his lips.

Rita stood at the foot of the makeshift bed. The boys had rolled towards each other and slept, breathing the same air, back and forth. Their feet stuck out from under the blankets. Rita bent and took hold of the covers.

"What are you doing?" Joseph whispered.

"I'm tucking them in."

Felix woke early. There were no curtains and the old panes of glass were buckled in places, making ripples on the sky that filled the window. The light in the room was new and hazy. The old down in the pillows had formed a mound on either side of his head and the slender shaft of a feather poked through the pillowcase. He pressed it back through the cotton. Luc was still asleep with his thumb near his open mouth. Felix turned back to the window and tried to piece together the events of the day before. It had all happened so quickly. They'd travelled so many miles and here they were. From the other side of the door he heard running water. Someone was up. Luc tapped him on the shoulder. "Are you awake?" he said. Felix rolled over. Luc yawned and rubbed his eyes with his fists. "This place is creepy," he said.

"I don't know," said Felix, looking at the ceiling, at a cobweb that drooped from the light fitting, "I like it."

Their rucksacks were propped against the wall and the side pocket of Luc's gaped open. He sat up and checked for his passport and wallet. Everything was there where it was meant to be. He folded the used train tickets and pushed them to the bottom of the bag. It was hard to believe that it was just two days ago that Felix had called. He'd sounded different, anxious, and they'd arranged to meet in their usual place, by the fountain. The sun had been hot and they'd moved into the shadow of the elevated concrete cube that was part of the Municipal Library. Luc remembered the urgency in Felix's voice.

"I can't go back," he said. "Will you come with me?"

"Where?" said Luc.

"I found this," said Felix. His hands shook as he held a guidebook out for Luc to see. The glue on the spine had dried and the pages were coming loose from the hard cover. From between the pages, he picked out a Polaroid: a far-off figure, a man in shorts, stood at the crest of an immense sand dune, knee-deep in coarse grass. Luc turned it over and written on the back in faded blue loops of handwriting was a single word.

"Is that the name of a town?" Luc asked.

"There's a train," said Felix. "I checked on the way."

"Wait," Luc stopped him, "where did you get this?"

"At the market," he said.

"And we just go?"

Luc remembered laughing. He remembered sneaking into their homes to pack a bag each, the wait in the station, then the night on the train. They had lain on bunks less than shoulder width apart with a soldier on the bunk below. His snores had rattled in time with the carriage while his belches filled the compartment with the smell of acrid yeast. When they arrived they looked for the bus station. Felix copied the name of the town from the back of the photo and showed it at the ticket office. They only had a few hours to wait. They bought sandwiches and watched passengers come and go until it was time for them to board.

Luc turned round and Felix had his back to him, the remains of his summer tan dark against the drape of the white sheet.

Rita wound a dishcloth round her hands and knocked on the bottom of the bread tin. Steam rose from the base of the loaf as it tumbled on to the cooling rack. It had rained in the night, melting the snow on the roof, and water dripped through the skylight so she placed a ceramic basin on the floor. She filled a pan from the tap, put it on the stove to boil, laid a blue cotton cloth across the table and went to dress.

The bedroom smelt stale. "Joseph," she said. "Joseph, wake up." Rita pushed open the windows then the shutters. "They could help us." Joseph stared up at Rita. His eyes were grey and watery, as if the colour had been drained from them. "Let's ask them to stay," she said.

"What are you talking about?" Joseph sat up in bed smoothing the wisps of hair across his head.

"The boys," said Rita, sitting on the edge of the bed. "Have you forgotten?"

"No, of course not." He pushed the bedcovers back, forcing her to move. "Just slow down," he said. Rita kept talking.

"There are so many things," she said, following him as he picked up clothes from the floor. "They could help us fix the place up."

"Why would they want to do that?"

She sat back down. Joseph sat next to her and pulled his socks on. Rita stroked his freckled shoulder, smoothed down his vest and passed him his shirt. "Will you ask them?" she said.

Felix dressed while Luc showered, then went to the kitchen where Rita and Joseph prepared breakfast. He sat at the far side of the table and Joseph put down plates, cups and knives in front of him. "How did you sleep?" he asked.

"Very well," said Felix.

Luc came out of the bathroom with a towel slung over his shoulder. "Me too," he said, stretching his arms above his head.

Rita cut a block of butter and put it on a saucer. She spooned jam into a bowl. "Please," she said, cutting into the fresh loaf and piling slices on the breadboard, "help yourselves." Joseph felt the side of the coffee pot, filled the cups and Rita stood back at the sink drinking her coffee. She watched Felix tame his black curls behind his ear and mop a berry from his white T-shirt. He chewed, looking down all the while. Luc looked around the room as he ate, taking eager bites of bread and smiling over at Rita between slurps of coffee. He looked younger than Felix. He tried to hide it with his black jeans and T-shirt. An attempt at sophistication, Rita thought, but the blonde hair sticking out in unruly clumps made him look like a schoolboy. But they can't be much older than that, she thought. As composed as Felix was, his porcelain skin gave him away.

"Are you on holiday?" Rita started. Joseph held up his hand and continued.

"Do you need work, a place to stay?"

Felix looked at Luc who shrugged. "We don't really have any plans," he said.

"Because I," he looked back at Rita, "we, can offer you work. There are repairs to be done."

Felix ran his finger over a knot in the table.

"It's very kind..." said Luc, picking at the crumbs on his plate.

"Go for a walk," said Joseph. "Have a look around. See what you think." He got up from the bench, leaning all his weight on the creaking table.

They followed the road round the edge of the forest until Luc stopped suddenly. The trees, which had bordered the path like a wall, broke into orderly lines along needle-covered peaks. Doors of light at the end of the furrows promised vastness. "Let's cut through," said Felix.

The deeper they went into the forest the fainter the path became and they weaved their way, following one chink of light then another, until the forest was behind them. Stepping out from the curtains of trees, they stood centre stage with the sea and sand for an audience. They drank in the bays and capes before them: folds and folds of snow-covered sand, mountains of it, and not a single person in sight.

Luc yelled as he ran, breaking the icy crust, flicking snow then sand with his heels. Felix followed. His torso moved faster than his legs and soon he was tumbling. He grabbed on to Luc and pulled him down, laughing. As they rolled and rolled, sand and snow filled their pockets and their shoes. It matted their hair. They clenched their eyes shut until they lay flat on their backs. Felix sat up and spat, coughed then spat again. He pulled his sleeve over his hand and wiped his mouth. "You go back," he said. "Tell them we'll stay."

"Now?" Luc shook the sand from his hair.

"It seems important to them."

"What about you?" said Luc. He stood and brushed

down his jeans. Felix blocked out the low sun behind him.

"I'll walk some more," he said.

Rita watched from the window as Joseph stopped chopping wood and went to meet Luc at the garden gate. She held the cloth mid circle on the plate, letting the water run over her wrists. Joseph shook Luc's hand, patted him on the back and handed him the axe.

"They've agreed." Joseph called as he came through the door. He threw his coat over the back of a chair and put his hands on Rita's waist. He kissed her neck.

"Thank you," she said. She pushed his arms away, picked up his coat and hung it in the porch. From the garden came the dunt and crack of the axe hitting wood and she buried her face in the folds of old sheepskin to hide her smile. The wood was damp but splitting easily enough and, stacked correctly, would be dry for next winter.

Luc added the logs to the pile and picked a fresh one to chop. As he swung the axe, he saw Felix in the road, cradling something at his chest. Luc jammed the blade in the log and ran to meet him. "Don't frighten it, Luc," said Felix and he pulled his coat tighter. "It's a cormorant, I think. It's caught up in fishing line."

Rita saw them coming and held the door open. She shook the flour from her apron and pushed the hair from her face with the back of her hand. "Luc, run and find Joseph," she said. Felix held the bird against the warmth of his chest, pointing the beak away from him. "Keep her eyes covered," said Rita, "and hold her firmly under your arm. We don't want her spreading those wings." She made comforting noises near the bird's head while they waited.

"Will she be okay?" Felix asked.

"I've seen worse."

Joseph burst into the room with Luc at his heels. "Where did you find her?" he said.

"At the edge of the forest," said Felix. He tightened his hold on the bird as Joseph touched the line wrapped tightly round its legs.

"By the lagoon?" said Joseph. He followed the line behind its neck and round its bill. "Shh now," he said, "I think we can get you out of this easily enough." He looked up at Rita. "There's no hook here, unless she's swallowed it."

"I'll get my sewing basket," said Rita. She took her basket from the sideboard and pulled out a small pair of scissors. A tangle of thread and wool came with them. Joseph waved his hand impatiently in her direction.

"Now Felix," he said, "be ready for her to flinch when I cut the line. Okay?"

"I'm ready."

Luc glanced at Felix. His shirt had come unbuttoned and his cheeks were flushed with concentration. Joseph slid the tip of the scissors under the line and made several cuts. He nudged the nylon free from the bird's legs and flexed its webbed feet then, breathing heavily, he gently unwound the line from its neck, feeding it between his fingers.

"Let's get it back to where you found it," said Joseph.

Rita walked in front with Felix. Joseph and Luc followed behind. They cut through the woods and down to the frozen waters of the lagoon. Felix took the bird close to the shore. He lowered it to the ground and, as soon as he loosened his grip, the bird flapped its great wings, ran clumsily on the crusts of snow then flew to the jagged branches of a dead tree. They stood and watched it flex and spread its wings, uncompromisingly black, against the mottled, white backdrop.

After lunch, Luc stacked the soup bowls and took them to the sink. "So," he said, "put us to work. Where can we start?" Joseph rubbed his beard and looked around the room.

"There's so much," he said.

"The skirting," said Rita. She pointed to the gaps above the floorboards. The furniture hid the fact that a finger width space ran around the bottom of the wall. Luc went closer. He felt the draught rushing in.

"You can smell the soil under the house," said Luc.

"It's a good place to start," said Joseph. He led them into the garden, to the shed at the side of the house and handed Luc a key. "There are tools in there and timber. I haven't looked for a while but there should be everything you need. Can you manage that?"

"Sure," said Luc, "no problem."

"I'll let you get on then," said Joseph and he walked out of the open gate, stopped for a second, then turned right. His coat was so long it dragged on the surface of the snow.

"At least he's put his boots on this time," said Luc and they watched him until he turned again.

"D'you know what you're doing?" said Felix. "Building I mean. Have you ever done anything like this before?"

"I take it you haven't."

"Never," said Felix.

"I've helped my uncle fix up his boat," said Luc. "Can't be so different."

The shed leaned to one side and the roof sagged in the middle. Luc tried the key. The padlock was frozen but the latch hung by a single screw so Luc worked his fingers behind it, pulled it loose and edged the door over a stone slab that had shifted in its foundations.

"Felix, come and look."

Felix peered round the door. "Jesus," he said. "Looks like someone's picked it up, given it a shake and tossed it back down." Luc loosened the tangle of tools, pulling at pieces of wood and half-empty tins of paint. He saw what he was looking for and took hold of the first plank, tugged it out and started to make a stack on the grass.

"Some of these are warped," said Luc. "We can't use them." He stepped over the mess and into the shed. At the back, boxes were piled as high as the roof. "How long have these guys been here?" he said. "Looks like they've still to unpack." A ceramic plaque hung from a nail. In relief was a town with its name running round the rim. Luc spelt it out to Felix. "Where is that?" he said.

"I don't know," said Felix. "I don't recognise it."

Between them they carried a toolbox into the house and measured the walls and the spaces they needed to fill then, on the back step, they cut the lengths of wood. Felix held the planks up against the wall while Luc hammered in an assortment of nails to keep them in place. They stood back. The wood gaped against the curve of the old plasterboard and the rusty saw had chewed the corners to pieces.

"It's an improvement," said Felix.

"You think?" said Luc. "I'm going to keep going."

While Luc clawed out nails Felix went into the kitchen where Rita was sweeping the floor and when she saw him she leaned the broom against the wall. Felix sat down. He rubbed his hands and put them between his thighs to warm them. Rita filled the kettle and lit the stove. She reminded him of his mother, her braid reaching to the knot in her apron, though his mother was slighter, bird-like. He thought of her in the sun-filled kitchen at home the day he left.

He had shut the door by pressing his palm flat on the wood above the handle to prevent the ricochet as it jumped into the lock. It was mid-morning but he knew his dad would be asleep, fully clothed, on the sofa in the living room. When Felix was small his dad would come off the night shift, take a shower and shut the bedroom door to ensure his hours of sleep but he was lazy now, settling for a few hours on the sofa, any time of day. Felix heard his mum in the kitchen. She tried to muffle the sounds of dishes chinking in the drying rack by doing everything slower but the volume of her care was unbearable. He was tired and wanted to get to his room.

"Felix, is that you?" His mum stood in the doorway drying her hands with a cloth. "Can I fry you some eggs?"

"I ate at the market, Mum. I just need to get some sleep." Felix left her standing in a shaft of bright morning light and went to his room at the end of the hall.

The day was warm already so he lay on top of the covers and was just drifting off to sleep, his mind unpacking fruit and vegetables, throwing boxes on an unsteady mountain of cardboard, when he heard his mother's voice, shrill and bothered. He pulled his knees up towards his chest and tucked his hands between his thighs but he couldn't close his eyes again. The curtains wafted in the breeze from the open window and he thought about how he used to illustrate their shouts, turn the scene into a comic strip in his head by drawing featureless outlines of his parents, sealing their words into speech bubbles. Felix got out of bed and walked down the hall. He knew which floorboards to step over so he wouldn't be heard.

His dad was too big for the kitchen. He was barefoot and pacing. His thick, dark hair was flat on one side and the lines from the corduroy cushions were imprinted on his cheek. He poured coffee into a delicate white cup. It looked like part of a doll's tea set in his clumsy hand. He was looking for a teaspoon but the cutlery drawer was sticking. And it was her fault. Felix watched his mother fuss her hair behind her ears and agitate the simmering pots on the stove. His dad set down the cup next to the sugar bowl and tossed in three heaped spoonfuls. The glass of violets Felix had brought home was where his mother had placed it, in the middle of the table. Felix stepped into the kitchen from the doorway. His dad looked at him and swiped. Glass and water shattered across the floor.

"Leave her alone," said Felix.

"Get back to your room," said his dad, pressing his blunt fingertips into Felix's chest.

"I said, leave her alone."

Felix looked up into his dad's watery, bloodshot eyes then he was falling backwards, stumbling against the kitchen table, grabbing on to the chair. It felt as light as a feather as Felix swung it into the air then something cracked. He didn't know if it was the wood splitting or bones breaking. He'd never hit anyone before. His dad stumbled and slid down the kitchen cupboards until he was slumped on the floor, touching at the trickle of blood on his forehead. The seat of the chair and its two front legs lay sprawled next to the broken glass. Felix was still holding the rest of it. He wasn't sure what to do. He looked at his dad. His scrunched up face was full of hate. His mum sobbed into her hands in the corner of the room. Felix dropped the chair, grabbed his shoes at the door and ran, only pausing long enough at the bottom of the stairs to pull them on.

His bike was where he'd left it just an hour before and he ran it along the road then jumped on and pedalled. He didn't have to think where he was going; he just hoped Luc was at home.

Rita put a cup in front of Felix and sat opposite him. "Are you okay?" she said. Felix stirred honey into his tea and licked the metallic sweetness from the spoon.

"Do you have children, Rita?"

"Otto. We had Otto. You remind me of him a little."

"Where does he live?"

Rita looked away. "He died, Felix. Otto died."

Luc started hammering.

"Come shopping with me," said Rita over the noise. "Luc can finish up. I'd like the company."

Felix looked at Luc to see if he'd heard but he was pulling out another nail. He put it between his lips at the corner of his mouth while he lined up the wood again and waved them away. "I'd like that," said Felix.

As they walked along the road their breath clouded in front of them but the sun was warm on Felix's face. Somebody was calling after them. It was a child's voice.

"Wait!"

Rita turned and saw the familiar small figure running towards them. "Wait," the boy called again, though she had already slowed her pace.

"I have shopping to do, Misha," Rita shouted, but he ran and caught up with them, jumping over potholes in the road. Misha pulled on Rita's hand. "Felix, meet Misha," said Rita. "Misha, this is Felix." Misha kept pulling at Rita. "What is it?"

"My mother," he said. Through a sparse grouping of pines, there stood two low apartment blocks. Misha pointed up at the second floor. From the balcony, a young woman with henna-red hair waved at them, a cigarette between her fingers.

"Coffee!" she called down.

They climbed the stairs and Misha's mother stood at the open door smoothing down her skirt and adjusting her tight blouse. "Come in, come in. A quick coffee." She smiled broadly. Rita noticed a gold tooth on one side, spaces on the other. She followed her into the small kitchen. "Please," she said, "have a seat." Rita eased herself behind the table followed by Felix, tucking the plastic checked tablecloth away from her knees. Everything was painted red: the walls, the chairs, the window frames. A poster of Kevin Costner hung on the back of the door. His name was written at an angle in one corner like a signature. "Handsome, don't you think?" Misha's mother stroked Kevin Costner's cheek and looked at Felix. "Like your friend?" She laughed and offered her hand. "Monica," she said. Rita held her fingers in a limp handshake then took a sip of the coffee that Monica put in front of her. Misha perched himself on the edge of a chair and sucked on a sugar lump. He reached for a second and his mother swatted at his hand. "That's enough. Now go and play."

Misha lay on his stomach driving a little car back and forwards over the same patch of carpet while Monica leaned against the work surface holding a fresh cigarette over the sink. "Misha talks a lot about you." She tapped ash into the plughole. "He likes helping you." On the windowsill sat a row of tangled objects: sea glass, stones, sticks and remnants of plastic bound together in bulbous formations with string.

"Did you make these?" Rita asked. Monica waved her hand and tutted.

"We collect things in the summer. I like to make jewellery." She pushed her hair behind her ear. An earring dangled to her shoulder. "Misha calls them his beach treasures." Rita drained her cup until the coffee grounds met her tongue.

"We should go now. Are you ready?" Felix nodded and drank up.

"Just a moment." Monica crossed the room to the window, picked up one of the objects and pushed it into Rita's hands. "Take one," she said. Tied together in Rita's palm was a piece of driftwood as smooth as a bone, a blue hair curler and a yellow plastic pipe. Rita put it in her pocket.

"Thank you."

"I see your husband out walking," said Monica, opening the door. "All times of day." Felix and Rita started down the stairwell. "And you," called Monica, leaning over the banister and pointing at Felix, "come to the bar. Bring your friend."

"Wait!" shouted Misha. He slipped out from behind his mother's legs and skipped down the stairs until he caught up with them and held on to Rita's string bag.

Felix followed Rita across the town square as she shopped for meat and eggs and vegetables that had been stored through the winter and Misha followed them both. He disappeared behind shelves then reappeared sucking a lollipop then ran ahead of them and hid, waiting for them to feign surprise when he jumped out from a shop entrance. Rita gave him a bag to carry and he dawdled behind them as she and Felix took the road home.

"What brings you here, Felix?" said Rita. "You're a long way from home."

Felix thought for a while about how to answer. He could tell her about the photo he'd found, how he'd looked the town up in an atlas, how it was as good a place as any. "I couldn't stay there," he said. Rita nodded. Misha skipped around them in a circle then fell behind again.

"Have you lived here long?" said Felix.

"A while," said Rita. "Like you, home was difficult. After Otto died…" she trailed off. "But I knew this place. I came on holiday as a child. My aunt kept a summer house. I think, sometimes, that we should have stayed."

"At home?" said Felix.

"It wouldn't have been any better, but yes."

"Rita, do you think it's wrong to leave your problems?" She stopped and faced Felix. He still had so much ahead of him.

"What's wrong for me, Felix," she said, "could be right for you."

Misha caught up with them and Rita took the bag from him and waved him off.

"Come to the bar tonight," they heard through the trees. It was Monica leaning over the balcony again. "And bring your friend!" she shouted. Rita laughed.

"She's keen," she said. "You should go. Spend time with people your own age."

As they walked through the gate Luc was carrying offcuts to the shed. "Back in time to help me clear up?" he said.

"You were doing such a good job," said Felix. Luc grinned.

"Come and see," he said. "It's not bad at all."

"Is Joseph back?" said Rita.

"He's inside."

Rita went in. Joseph was sitting at the table. She filled the fruit bowl with apples and hung her bag on the door handle. "I met Misha's mother today," she said. Joseph closed his book and took his glasses off. "You know, the little boy that follows me, I've told you about him. Her name's Monica," Rita said. "We could invite her over." Joseph rubbed his beard, looked around the room. Rita followed his gaze. "You're right. Maybe when it's cleaned up a bit." She cleared the dishes from the table. "But the boys should meet some young people."

"I've given them some money to go out," said Joseph. He put his hand on Rita's waist, stopping her in her tracks. "I thought that we could talk." She looked down at him then broke free.

"Yes," she said, "maybe we could."

Rita fished in her pocket for the present Monica had given her. The string had come undone and she pulled it out along with the piece of wood and the curler. She could fix it later, she thought.

It was already dark when they headed along to the town. The sky was bright with stars and the air was crisp. Felix had wanted to get the fire going before they left but Rita hurried them out with warnings to keep warm as a snowfall was forecast.

The bar was the only one in the town square. In the window, its name flashed on and off in neon. Luc held the door open for Felix. They could hear music behind the velvet curtain, hung to keep the cold out. "You go first." Felix whispered. Luc found the opening in the curtain and slipped through. The room was warm and thick with smoke. He pulled his coat off and slung it over his shoulder. Booths ran along one side and at the back coloured lights moved across an empty dance floor. Monica jumped down from a stool at the bar.

"You came," she said. "Florian, drinks for my guests please."

"What can I get you boys?" The barman was a head taller than Luc and his arms were dense with muscle.

"Two beers, please." Luc dug into his pocket for the money Joseph had given them but Monica put out her hand.

"My treat," she said.

"You old enough?" said Florian, reaching up for two glasses. His shirtsleeve pulled up to reveal a tattoo of a heart with a feather piercing a hole in its middle. He poured the drinks, tapping his fingers to the music on the silver beer tap. "Take a seat." He nodded to an empty table. "I'll bring these over."

They slid around either side of the table and met at the curve of the bench. Their booth was sandwiched between a group of girls giggling and watching their every move and a couple so wound around each other it was hard to tell where one began and the other ended. One of the girls stuck her head round the divide. Her eyes were playful, her smile confident and teasing.

"Come and sit with us," she said.

"Leave them, Audra." The barman pushed the drinks across the table. "Let them drink in peace." He gave her a friendly clip around the ear.

"They wanted us out of the way, didn't they?" Felix said, thinking about Joseph and Rita in the house alone.

"Relax. We may as well enjoy ourselves." Luc lifted his glass and, with a nod to Felix, gulped his beer down. "Shall we play pool?" He slid his way around the bench and the girl from the next booth pounced like a kitten.

"Let's play doubles," she said. She pulled at the shoulder of one of her friends. "This is Rasa," said Audra. Rasa's eyelashes propped up a heavy, dark fringe. She took the cue that Audra handed to her and turned to Luc.

"Spots or stripes?" said Rasa.

"Stripes," said Luc. "Felix, that okay with you?"

Felix shrugged. Audra pulled a coin from the back pocket of her tight jeans, dropped it in the slot and pushed the drawer into the table with the heel of her hand. The balls gave a low rumble then clattered into the tray. She filled the triangle with red and yellow balls then rearranged the colours, lifted the black from the middle, slid the triangle back and forward and lined the space up with the chalk dot on the table. She took Luc by the wrist and thrust the white ball into his palm.

"You break," said Audra.

Luc rested his hip on the edge of the table and belted the white ball into the cluster. The balls scattered in every direction but nothing went down. He laughed and handed the cue to Felix. Audra pursed her lips and pocketed one after the other. Felix watched her strut round the table. Her blouse was too old for her, he thought, and she wore too much make-up, but she was pretty, in a brazen kind of way. Finally, a red ball bounced on the corner of a pocket and trembled to a standstill. The barman gave a whistle behind them. He set out four shot glasses and filled them from a show-off height. "Vodka. On the house," he said.

"Thanks, Florian." Audra gave him a wink. Luc reached for a glass and nudged Felix towards the table.

"You're up."

Felix moved gracefully and the others stood back as he cleared the table. Audra knocked back her vodka and lit herself a cigarette. "Another game?" she said. She went through the setting up routine and just as Rasa was about to break Audra tossed her cue on to the table knocking the balls out of position. "It's my favourite song," she said. "Come and dance." She took Luc's hand. Rasa picked at a peeling sticker on her cue.

"D'you want another game, Felix?"

"Can we just sit for a while?"

Rasa looked relieved and he carried their glasses back to the booth. Florian came round with a tray of candles, lighting one before placing it in the centre of the table. Felix pushed the softened rim and a dribble of molten wax ran down the side and pooled in its holder. They sat side by side and watched Luc and Audra. The couple in the next booth unwrapped themselves from each other and went up to join the dancing.

"She's got a boyfriend, you know," said Rasa. "He's in the army." Felix looked at Audra moving around Luc on the dance floor. "He trusts her. They've always been together," said Rasa. Felix cleared his throat to speak over the music.

"What about you?" he said. "Have you got a boyfriend?"

"Not any more." Felix swigged his beer. "I have a baby, a son," she said. Felix opened his eyes wide and swallowed his mouthful. They watched the dancers throw back their heads in laughter. "And I write stories." Rasa shifted herself round to get Felix's full attention.

"What about?" he asked. She tucked her hair behind her ear.

"There's one about a man who lost an umbrella given to him by a lover." Rasa drew lines, one way then the other, in a wet patch on the table. "This umbrella held the memories of their relationship and, when he lost the umbrella, he lost the memories too."

"It sounds sad. Are they all sad?"

"No, there's another one about a girl who meets a boy," Rasa said. She smiled at Felix. "He doesn't talk about love from the first moment like the other boys."

"What did he talk about?" said Felix.

"Horses."

Felix laughed. He noticed the gap between Rasa's front teeth. They leaned back against the cushioned bench and looked over at the dance floor in time to see Luc clasp his hands round Audra's waist and pull her towards him. Audra stood on her tiptoes and offered her lips to Luc.

Felix pushed past Rasa. "Where are you going?" she said. But he was out the door, the cold hitting him like a wall. He didn't know if it was the alcohol or the cold but his legs were not following a straight path. He turned his collar up round his neck and dug his hands into his pockets. It was snowing lightly and the flakes settled on his left side as he followed the road back to the house.

Joseph was pacing the room. He'd wanted to talk but now, when it came to it, he didn't know where to start. "I don't know what you want me to do," he said.

"You could take your coat off," said Rita.

Joseph looked at Rita sitting in the armchair, sewing in the candlelight. He imagined roots sprouting from under her skirt, through the legs of the chair, deep into the ground, securing her to that spot by the fireplace for evermore where the grate lay empty. "You'll strain your eyes," said Joseph. "Or prick your finger."

"I could unpick stitches with a blindfold on, Joseph." Rita laid her sewing carefully on the worn arm of the chair. "Let's talk then," she said.

"I don't know what to say Rita. We came here. We started a new life."

"We ran away," said Rita.

"Could you have stayed in that house?" Joseph slammed his hand on the table. "Could you have walked past his room every day and not seen him hanging there?" Rita let out a cry. "If you want to talk about what happened, that's what happened." Joseph started to pace the room, steadying himself on the furniture. Rita breathed deeply.

"I want to talk about why it happened. Why we couldn't…"

"I don't have any answers!" yelled Joseph.

Rita felt herself shrinking into the chair. He was taking up all the oxygen in the room, sucking it up, and replacing it with his anger. She wanted to float to the surface and gasp at a pocket of sweet air. Air filled with memories. Otto in shorts aged five with muddy knees and rosy cheeks. Otto aged twelve, grinning, on his bike, one foot on the ground. Joseph looked at Rita and spoke softly. "I don't have any answers, Rita." She shook her head.

"I don't expect you to."

Joseph rifled through the cupboards until he found a bottle of cognac. He twisted off the cap and gritty crystals of alcohol fell into his hand. He took two glasses from the sink, sloshed out their dregs and poured a generous measure into each. Rita stood, pulled the blanket from the back of the chair and draped it round her shoulders. They both sniffed at their glass then took a mouthful.

"I dream that I wake up," said Rita, "that I go through to the kitchen and people have started moving in." She tightened her grip on her shawl. "In the dream I've slept through it all and there's nothing I can do. They don't understand what I'm saying and I can't phone anyone because they've taken the list of phone numbers from the wall." Joseph filled his glass again. "They even put place mats on the table and there's a child sleeping in my bed. I gather up a small bag of my things, get dressed and decide to accept the situation."

"And what?"

"I stand outside, watching the flat revolve like a music box." Rita sipped at her drink, relishing the burn in her throat and the warmth travelling to her stomach. Joseph ran his hands through his beard and sat down at the table.

"He was nearly an adult Rita. We couldn't possibly have known everything about him."

Rita glared at him then disappeared into the bedroom. Joseph filled both glasses again and listened to objects landing hard on the floor. Rita returned carrying a book. She put it on the table and Joseph prodded it with his finger. "What is this?" he said then clasped his hand over his mouth. The word "PRIVATE" was written across the red leather binding. The block capitals and cross-hatching that filled each letter were, undoubtedly, the graphics of his son. "Have you had this all this time?" Joseph's voice shook. "Have you read it?" Rita placed her hand on the book.

"I've never opened it."

The book lay between them offering everything and nothing. Its red cover had faded and the shadow of two smaller books had left their mark. Joseph pictured it sitting, forgotten, in a sunlit pile on Otto's desk. His room was at the front of the house, facing west. Joseph remembered calling Otto for dinner. He went upstairs to call again. Lit from behind was Otto's suspended silhouette.

Joseph's chair screeched against the floorboards and fell back as he stood bolt upright. "It's too late," he shouted and threw the book across the room. Pages, postcards and tickets fluttered to the ground. Rita ran to save them. She moved around the room gathering the remnants in her skirt.

"Help me, Joseph." Rita's face was wet with tears. "Help me." Joseph stayed where he was, unable to take his eyes off her, unable to move. She felt warmth at her temple. "The candle" she whispered. Flames were creeping up the wall like rampant ivy.

Felix saw a light flicker in the window. It was too bright, too agile. He started to run. A bucket at the side of the house had filled with rainwater from the cracked gutter. He lifted it with both hands and kicked the door. The overspill soaked his ankles. The light was dancing now and Joseph was gracelessly hitting at it. He'd taken the rug from the floor and was beating at the window but the flames, tamed for a second, leapt with renewed energy. He hit again and a pane of glass shattered. Felix limped across the room. The bucket knocked against his knees and he took hold of its base and swung an arc of water at the flames.

Joseph turned to him, watermarks mushrooming on his suede coat. The bedraggled curtain dropped to the ground, its singed edges still glowing. Felix stepped forward and stamped on it, grinding the soles of his boots into the broken glass. Rita hid her face in her hands. "It's a mess, Felix." She muffled her sobs then wiped her hands on her cheeks and looked at him. "It's all such a mess."

Joseph flung the rug into the corner of the room where it landed in awkward folds. He watched Felix comfort Rita. The solitary curtain billowed pathetically in gusts of freezing air. He should patch the window, but the door lay open, inviting him into the night and he shut it behind him, gently, as if he were afraid of waking someone.

"He's soaking, Rita. I'll go after him." Felix started towards the door but Rita took his hand and held it in both of hers.

"He'll come back," she said and brushed at something on his cheek. "He always does."

"Jesus, what happened here?" Luc took in the wet heap of material and broken glass, the shadows of smoke etched on the wall. "Are you okay?" He went to them both but Felix put out his hand to stop him. Rita looked at the sodden pages on the floor, words lapping over one another.

"I'm going to bed. I've had enough."

Luc waited for Rita to close the bedroom door.

"Where's Joseph?"

Felix fetched the broom from the cupboard and started sweeping. Luc grabbed the handle.

"What happened here?"

"I've no idea. The place was on fire when I came back."

"I pushed her away, Felix. You know that don't you?"
"What do I care?"
"We were just having fun. She showed me a photo of her soldier boyfriend on his motorbike." Luc held his arms out to show the bulk of the boyfriend and grinned. He slid his hand round the back of Felix's neck and gently gripped his hair.

The rising sun blushed over the ice, the morning mist absorbing its glare. Felix slapped his mittened hands together and hopped from one foot to the other. Luc gripped the flask of coffee Rita had made, his teeth chattering.

"Come on you two."

They followed Joseph. A layer of powder snow loosely covered the ice. Their footsteps vanished in little gusts as soon as they were made. Luc tried to skid but the unpolished surface refused his glide.

"This'll do."

Felix looked behind them. He couldn't see the shore. The cloud had settled around them like a protective layer of cotton wool. The lake felt inconceivably flat underfoot. And still. He thought about the movement below, the life, and felt his legs weaken behind his knees. Joseph laid down his bag letting the sides fall open.

"Here, hold this." He handed Luc a tool the length of his leg with a torturous looking corkscrew. Luc turned the handle and watched the blades turn like a helter-skelter. Joseph was laying his equipment out on the ice like a surgeon preparing for an operation.

"Luc, you drill a hole."

Luc and Felix looked at each other suppressing a laugh and Luc stabbed at the ice with the drill. It skidded to one side. Joseph planted his feet hip width apart, raised the drill and made one solid jab. The drill end was encased in the ice.

"Now, Felix, you hold it steady while Luc drills. It'll warm you up."

They watched the blades break the surface and churn deeper in search of the other side. Luc's hand slipped on the handle.

"I think that's it."

"Felix, take this chisel and we'll make the hole bigger."

Luc pulled the drill out and Felix chipped away at the sides. The water lapped as he worked. Joseph assembled the rod and set up three small stools. They threaded the bait on to the hooks and dropped the weights into the water.

"Now what do we do?" whispered Felix.

"We wait."

"What's that noise?" They all concentrated on a low barely audible beat. The sound was distant but the more he listened the more Felix felt it enter him until his breathing fell in time.

"Ah, it attracts the smelt. The fishermen beat sticks together under the water to lull the fish."

"Hypnotise them?" Luc blew into his hand and rubbed his leg.

"I suppose so." Joseph looked at his watch.

"Felix, will you light the stove. Let's get ready to eat."

The ice at the edge of the shore had frozen mid wave. It was messy and uneven. There were ridges high enough for Rita to lean on. She pushed her hands deep into her pockets. She'd said goodbye to the others and turned right towards the sea. The lagoon was too stagnant for her today, the sitting and waiting too difficult. She needed the deep, full-throated roar of the ocean. The waves had frozen mid turn. Deeper water beat against the solid crests spitting cubes of ice on to the sand. She remembered the rhythm of the loom, shooting the shuttle through the opening of the warp and packing the yarn hard into the woven fabric. The coordination of hand and foot as she lifted her knee to operate the pedal, the soft wooden clunk, solid and reassuring. Today there was amber. Rita took one glove off to pick up the tiny rust-coloured shards. Some days there was plenty then the wind changed and weeks past with nothing. They would fish for a while, Joseph and the boys, then Luc had mentioned something about meeting a friend. She couldn't remember their name, maybe Joseph would know. It had been a while now. She turned back to the house.

A figure bounced and waved on the far side of the lagoon. Felix stopped in his tracks and dropped his bag. Its fabric muffled the chime of glass against glass as it hit the ground.

"Careful," said Luc, checking the bottles were intact.

"You arranged this with her, didn't you?" Felix pushed the hair off his forehead, fingers catching in his dark curls. Luc swung the bag over his shoulder.

"She's harmless, come on." He gave Felix a gentle shove. "You might even enjoy yourself."

Felix turned his back to the water, blocking Luc's view of Audra.

"She's a flirt," he said under his breath and scuffed his boot on the stones.

"You like Rasa though, don't you?"

Felix caught up with him. "I like her stories."

The path narrowed and Felix fell behind. Audra was still hopping up and down further along the shore. Behind her, Rasa hunched over some bags and as she stood, her black hair swung, glinting in the watery light. The ground was hard underfoot and the sun hung heavy in the sky.

"Come on, hurry up, we need you to collect wood," Audra called out as soon as they were in earshot and Luc ran the last stretch to greet them. They spread out into the trees, ducking under low branches, gathering twigs to get the fire started and dense branches to keep it going.

"Where's your son today, Rasa?" Luc called over.

"He's with my mother." Rasa added a heavy stick to Felix's armful as he passed her. Audra lifted stones from the shore, arranged them in a circle, and separated the wood into fast and slow burning. Felix knelt between the piles.

"Has anyone got any paper?"

Rasa took a notebook from her pocket. "It's full of lists," she said, "not worth remembering." Grouping the back pages, she ripped hard, pulling the binding thread free, and gave the handful to Felix. He scrunched the pages into balls and carefully stacked smaller sticks around them.

"You'll need to break up some of those bigger branches." He said to Luc over his shoulder as he lit the paper.

Luc made a mock salute behind Felix's back and picked up the largest branch. Holding it in one hand, he stamped near the middle. His foot slid down the bark and he stumbled towards the fire. Audra laughed. Luc threw the branch to one side, rolled the bottles of beer out of the backpack and snagged the caps off on the edge of a rock. He passed them round.

"So what have we got to eat?"

"Sausages," Audra said and she tipped a greasy parcel from her bag on to the ground.

Felix picked out four thin sticks from the pile and whittled the bark away to a sharp point with his penknife. They pierced the sausages, stuffed the meat on to the stick and held them over the flames until their skins were hissing and spitting fat on to the burning wood. Felix shivered as a cold breeze caught his back. He tucked his T-shirt into his jeans.

"Maybe Rasa could tell us a story."

"I can't, not just like that."

"Go on, a short one," said Luc.

"Don't hold it right in the flame." Audra pushed Luc's arm. "It'll burn." Rasa shifted her weight on the rock, "I'll tell you a kind of story. But you have to promise not to laugh."

"We won't."

"Okay," Rasa cleared her throat and pointed along the shore, "Picture in that tree."

"Which tree?"

"Quiet Luc."

"The bare one," she pointed, "close to the water. Picture a bird on its lowest branch, with gleaming golden feathers like a circus performer's headdress. Can you all see it?" she checked. "Now picture it dancing, pirouetting along the slope of the branch."

"Is it going to fall off?" Luc said, giggling behind his hand.

"Now do you see the other one? On the higher branch, another bird of paradise, the same outrageous crown of feathers. He's moving exactly in time with his friend on the branch below."

"And can you hear them, calling to each other, in throaty whistles? As the dance steps get faster the calls come quicker." Rasa stopped to let them listen. "An audience gathers." She lowered her voice. "A crowd of young males fluffing their immature pale feathers." Felix looked from the tree to Rasa. Her lips were such a deep red. He wondered if she was wearing lipstick.

"Wait, a female has joined the crowd. The dance becomes frantic." She paused. "They slow now, the dance turning into a shuffle and they drag their legs as if crippled. They bow their heads and their feathers droop in filmy clouds of yellow, but it's not over." Felix took the stick from Rasa's hand. She barely noticed. "Watch them tuck their legs into their chest, their eyes glass over, their mouths gape open. They start to tremble and shiver, and the crowd wonders if they are going to die right in front of them. And then," she lifted her hands above her head, "they raise their feathers in a gorgeous fountain of cascading plumes." Rasa tumbled her hands down to her feet then sat up straight. "Until they no longer resemble birds but some wild, exotic blossom." She smiled at her captive audience. "They hold this pose then move, exhausted, to another branch to recover because this is only an interval." Then, leaning in, she whispered, "Act two will start in a minute."

Luc held his stick between his knees to applaud while Felix and Audra clapped their free hands against their legs.

"Okay, my friends, let's eat," said Audra. She passed her stick to Rasa and pulled a sheet of cardboard from her bag. She folded it in half, first one way then the other, tore it along its softened creases and laid the four rectangles in front of her. She rummaged again in the bag, brought out a jar and spooned a dollop of mustard on to the corner of each plate.

Rasa took a dark loaf of bread from a paper bag and Felix handed her the knife. She cut four thick slices, passed them round and they ate greedily, smearing mustard, mopping the meaty juices before throwing the makeshift plates on the fire. Felix licked his fingers, took a long final swig of his beer and ran flapping towards the tree, cawing like a crow. Luc laughed.

"What are you doing?" he called after him. Felix clambered up and straddled a high branch, leaning back against the trunk. He breathed in deeply, filling his lungs.

"Come on up."

"He's crazy." Audra huffed, following Luc and Rasa. They climbed to where Felix sat, perched in the branches. The view hung in horizontal stripes: lagoon, trees, dunes, sea.

"Let's not leave," said Rasa, "till the sun touches the horizon."

Rita whipped the covers back, letting them fall in a heap at the end of the bed. Joseph pulled his knees up to his soft belly and wrapped his arms round his sagging chest. "Get up, Joseph."

"It's freezing, woman."

"I want to do something with these. Now." She held, with both hands, a pile of paper. "I saved what I could and set them out to dry last night but look." Rita pulled a buckled page up for Joseph to see. The ink had slid to one corner forming an iridescent border. "I just need to do something with them, and you're coming with me." Rita prised his hand away from his body and pulled at him as if rousing a child.

"Okay, okay." He swung his feet on to the cold floorboards and reached down for the rumpled clothes he'd climbed out of, cold and damp from fishing. "Let me get dressed."

The last of the ice had broken into a heap that snaked along the shore and with each wave, the fragments of ice shuffled over each other, ringing like tiny bells. Rita pulled a handful of pages from her pocket and threw them away from herself, into the air.

"Wait." Joseph picked a page off the wet sand and started folding it. "Let's sail them out." He took Rita's hand, "Is that okay?" She nodded.

Joseph folded the paper in half and, resting it on

his thigh, brought the top corners to meet each other. Then, with his thumb and forefinger, he lifted the bottom of the sheet and folded one half to the front and the other behind.

"It looks like a hat."

Joseph looked her calmly in the eye, "It's a boat. Help me fold the rest of them."

They made a small fleet with the intact pages and tucked the damaged sheets into their fragile hulls. Rita knelt at the water's edge and collected the boats in her skirt. When all the pages were gone, Joseph crouched next to her.

"We'll have to just toss them in over the ice."

"They'll capsize."

"It's fine."

Joseph took a handful of boats, leaned over the ice and threw them gently into the water, one by one. They tipped and bounced against the waves. A few bobbed further out. Rita took the hem of her skirt and stood, flicking the remaining few into the water. They stood for a moment until Rita turned, one foot catching in her sunken footprint.

They climbed back up the crest of the dune. Joseph gave Rita his hand and helped her over the steep edge. Branches and twigs had collected, woven and matted in the space between the trees ending and the land falling away to sand. Joseph fished a stone from his pocket, turning it over in his fingers.

"You know male penguins start collecting pebbles at the nesting site before the females arrive." He held the stone out to Rita. "They look for the prettiest pebbles to woo their bride to be."

"I'm too old for this, Joseph."

"Rubbish." He started to kneel and Rita took his outstretched hand. The pebble caught between their palms. "Lie down with me."

As they stretched themselves out on the mattress of sticks, the wind shrank to a whistle through the grass. Rita pulled her woollen hat further over her ears and shuffled into the bulk of Joseph. Resting their chins on folded arms they watched the waves, their breathing falling in time then out again. They thought they saw the paper boats cresting the waves, breaking up and dissolving.

"It's been a long time since we came down here at night," Joseph said. "Remember the night the waves were glowing violet? You explained it away. Jellyfish, you said. I'd like to see that again. With you." Joseph leaned in and as Rita turned towards him, they met in a kiss. It could have been a kiss from years before but Rita felt the cold of Joseph's lips, the air on her face and the twigs scratching through her tights. She tried to give in to the warmth of their conjoined breaths. She tried to see the darkness as comforting but she broke away and from the corner of his eye Joseph saw Rita wiping her lips with the edge of her sleeve.

Felix and Luc stood at the top of the steps to the town hall next to a boxed-in noticeboard. Behind the glass hung a poster of Meryl Streep nestled into Clint Eastwood's shoulder. The town square sloped away from them. It was full of people milling around the dirty remains of shovelled snow. A van selling popcorn blared a crackly Macarena from its rooftop speaker.

"There they are," Luc pointed.

Joseph and Rita walked past the row of closed shops that lined the square. His coat brushed sluggishly against her woollen skirt. Luc waved but they didn't see him. As they passed the van, Joseph pulled Rita towards him with one hand on her waist then spun her away, keeping hold of her hand. He pulled her back towards him.

"Don't do that again," Rita said and stepped away from him as a couple passed them arm in arm. "There's Monica," Rita whispered loudly. "Who's she with?"

"Must be a boyfriend," said Joseph.

Monica looked over her shoulder and winked.

Joseph's eyes lit up as he saw Felix and Luc coming down the steps to meet them. "Ah good, you remembered."

Luc dug in his pockets but Joseph held his arm. "My treat, I invited you." He put some coins in Luc's hand. "Why don't you run down and get some popcorn. You'd like some wouldn't you, Rita?" They stood on the steps watching Felix and Luc make their way against the flow of the crowd.

"Don't be long," Joseph called out after them.

Felix and Luc returned laden with plastic bags of popcorn knotted at the top.

"Is everything okay?" Luc looked past Rita. Joseph was leaning towards the cashier. "Did he fix the window?"

"No. I patched it with cardboard." She took a bag

from Felix. "Maybe you can help him tomorrow." Joseph hurried towards them waving pink tickets in the air. "Come on, let's not miss the start."

In the warm, still auditorium the smell of smoke drifted from Felix's and Luc's clothes. They took their seats as the curtains opened and the lights dropped. Coughs bounced off the pine-clad walls and mingled with the rustle of wrappers. Felix leaned forwards to take his coat off and glanced at Luc, Rita and Joseph, their faces lit by the screen. He took a fistful of salty popcorn and, nudging Luc with his elbow, nodded along the row. Joseph held Rita's hand in her lap, their fingers intertwined.

The bed was cold and Rita rubbed her feet against the sheets to warm them. Her body wasn't ready for sleep. She hitched her nightgown up over her hips and leaned towards Joseph.

"Aren't you tired?" He said, smiling.

"Not yet."

"Well, I'm out of practice."

"Let's see if I can remind you then," she said. And after, while he slept, Rita lay listening to his snores rumbling softly in the space between them.

She lay like this until she heard the first bird call and she knew then that she couldn't stay. Her bag lay at the bottom of the cupboard in a pile of shoes and boots, and she filled it with clothes. She held a pen over a piece of paper before settling for a single word, "sorry", laid it on the bed and crept out of the house.

Joseph patted his hand on the mattress next to him

and found the note in Rita's place. He stared at the word, the carefully written letters. The weight of sleep fell away.

"Damn her," he said.

He threw back the blankets, pulled on his ancient sheepskin coat and grabbed the axe from behind the door. It had been Rita's idea to plant the tree, a eucalyptus. He'd told her not to put it so close to the house. Over the years, the tree had grown tall and spindly and every wind that blew whipped its branches against the kitchen window. It only took two blows of the axe to take it down. Joseph rubbed his forehead with the back of his hand and looked at the pathetic ragged stump.

She'd run out just when he could see an end, or a beginning. It had been a long silence. Occasionally he had thought they were at peace but these boys, Felix and Luc, had stirred up years of buried words that had bubbled up to the surface and burst against the walls of their neglected house.

He crossed the single road on the spit and took the track through the woods, his footsteps cushioned by fallen needles. He could make out birdsong muffled by the wind and his old-man breathing.

When they'd moved to this ribbon of land it was to make a new start and they would come and bed down in the forest, wrapped in each other, staring at the sky through the swaying treetops and listening to the waves.

Joseph came out of the woods and stood knee-deep in the seagrass that bound the sand together. The wind swirled the remaining wisps of grey hair round his cold scalp and heavy raindrops pockmarked the sand below him. He imagined she was there, a lone figure, walking towards the shore. He felt her name swell in his throat and he yelled, stretching the two halves of her name across the sand to the water's edge. And he was running, running down the dunes, planting his heels in the slope, breaking the smooth surface with each stride. His body creaked and lurched under its own weight.

Rita sheltered from the morning chill in the small waiting room. The bus timetable was hand-painted in blue on the whitewashed wall, the traced pencil lines of the letters still visible in places. She would go to the last town on the list, the end of the line. From there, she wasn't sure. Beside the door stood a pregnant woman, her mint green dress taut over her belly. She caught Rita's gaze and took her son's hand, pulling him towards her bare legs. At the other end of the bench, a man rolled up a bus ticket and, looking at Rita, used it to clean his ear.

"What time is it?" he said.

"I don't know," she shrugged.

It had been dark and raining when she left the house but now a wash of light seeped over the horizon. A driver approached the dormant bus. The doors let out a sharp intake of breath, snapped open and, with a deep sigh, closed behind him. He flicked on his overhead light, revved the engine and let it rumble as he sorted the change for the day. He checked his watch and nodded to the queue at the door.

Rita took a seat near the front and put her bag by the window. Hot air was blowing from the heaters and she took her coat off, folding it so the lining faced out, and put it on the shelf overhead. A shower of coins fell from her pockets. On her knees, she picked up the money, a shard of pottery, and there was something else. She reached further under the seat pulling her hand back sharply as her fingertips touched the hot radiator. She could see the yellow plastic and reached further until her hand felt the ragged seams of the pipe.

"Beach treasure," she whispered.

A girl started to sit in the seat next to her. Tinny music escaped from her earphones. Rita pushed past her. "I need to get off, sorry." She ran as far as she could through the town then walked, her bag bumping against her leg.

The sun shone brightly now and, as she turned along the coast road, she saw a familiar cluster of people gathered on the shore. They linked hands and formed a circle.

"Felix, Luc!" she cried out as she stepped heavily across the sand.

"Rita," Felix waved her towards her. "Come on."

"Sing with us," Monica shouted over the sound of breaking waves.

Rita dropped her bag on the sand and took her place in the chain that moved around Misha in the centre. He laughed as they threw him in the air, clapping and cheering. "Is Joseph at home?" Rita called to Luc.

"He went out before breakfast. We thought he

was looking for you." The laughter fell from his face. "Where were you?"

"I should find him." Misha hugged her legs and she bent to kiss his forehead, "Happy birthday."

As Rita went further into the forest, the ground piled up on either side of the path in steep humps like magnified ripples, pinned in place by pine trees. Lichen hung from branches like seaweed at low tide. Beads of sweat formed on Rita's brow. She followed his usual paths, stopping to call his name until she heard his voice, muffled but unmistakable.

"Joseph, are you there?" Rita stepped over the moss. A fallen tree had pulled up a scab of earth the length and breadth of its roots. Joseph was hunkered behind the knotted wall, talking softly, rubbing one hand in the other. Rita placed a hand on his shoulder.

"I've been looking for you."

Joseph looked up at her. He put his hand over hers. "You've found me."

Rita drew her heavy skirt round her legs and sat down next to him. Raindrops had collected in cobweb hammocks woven between the roots.

"Are you ready to go?"

"I think I might be." But neither made a move to rise. "Do you remember Rita, how Otto would rock himself to sleep?" Joseph clasped his hands over his ears and shook his head from side to side. Rita grabbed his arm and steadied him. A tear ran down her cheek. "He didn't want me to comfort him."

"I know. I know."

"Then he would sing to himself, so loudly. He argued with me, even in his sleep."

"Joseph."
"Yes."
"Let's go."

"Race you to the boat," Felix called over his shoulder as he ran through the woods to the shore. He jumped into the boat.

"Cheat," Luc shouted. "You're not meant to get in yet."

"I'm not that heavy," Felix laughed, picking the oars from under the seat. Luc loosened the rope and shoved the boat into the water, freeing it from the sand.

"I suppose you want me to row too," said Luc.

Felix passed him the oars and lay back on a folded tarpaulin, hands behind his head.

"Should we have gone with her?"

Luc rested the oars in the rowlocks and pulled the water back, gliding them out into the lagoon. "To look for Joseph?" He held the paddles on the surface of the water. "No. She'll find him." Luc pulled on one paddle and spun the boat. "They need to be alone though, Felix. Are you ready to move on?"

"You remember my sister don't you?"

"Of course, how could I forget?" Julie was older than Luc and she and her friends would hang around whispering and giggling every time he walked past. He would feel his cheeks redden as he came near them and there was nothing he could do to stop them. Julie called him pretty and wound her fingers in his curls. Once she'd tried to kiss him on the lips then laughed as he turned his face to avoid her.

"I'm sure she wouldn't mind us turning up there for a while."

"Hasn't she got a houseful? How many kids has she got now? And what about the husband?"

"Four. And Bruno's okay. They'd be glad of the help."

Julie had married a farmer and moved out of town into his sprawling farmhouse. They'd visited when she was pregnant with her first child. The house was overrun with animals and he remembered Julie crying when Bruno was out in the fields about the workload and how difficult it was going to be with a baby on top of everything else. She'd patted her stomach and groaned but Felix told her she looked beautiful and he meant it. Her hair was thick and glossy and her skin tanned from working outside.

He remembered the way she'd held her back as she led them into the barn that joined on to the farmhouse, the way she sighed as she looked around the vast space that was filled with rows and rows of metal shelving units. She took them down an aisle and pulled down a box, tipping it to show them its contents. It was full to the brim with an assortment of castors. She pulled down another box. Cable ties. Another one. Door handles. And on it went. "It's all catalogued," she said.

They followed her up a wooden staircase to a mezzanine stacked with items too big for boxes: skis, tennis racquets, picture frames. She opened a trunk and photographs slid on to the floor. She started to bend to pick them up.

"I'll get them," said Luc. He picked up the handful

of photographs and flicked through them. A smiling group outside a snow-covered chalet, a child blowing out candles on a cake, a sunset. "Who are these people?" said Luc.

"I have no idea," said Julie.

"Does Bruno?"

"No, it doesn't matter who they are to him," said Julie. "It doesn't matter."

Luc closed the lid of the trunk. A black Labrador bounded up the steps and started to lick Julie on the calf. "Okay, okay," she said. "I'll feed you."

Felix focused on the red clouds behind his eyelids and sunk into the warmth of the sun on his face. He was flying over the apartment block he grew up in. He circled the building, heard his mother's voice. His bedroom window was wide open, curtains flapping in the wind, the bed freshly made. "What's your favourite smell?" he said.

"Freshly sharpened pencils," said Luc.

Felix laughed, "What colour?"

"Blue, of course." Luc dipped his hand in the water and flicked some over Felix. "I packed our bags already."

"Where are they?"

"I left them by a tree."

Felix sat up. "You better get rowing then," he said, "before you forget which one."

They heaved the boat on to the sand and walked into the forest. Luc stopped to get his bearings then led them to the clearing and the tree with the markings he knew he'd recognise again.

"Cat's eyes," said Felix, pointing at the knots high on the trunk. Their rucksacks were tucked between its roots where Luc had left them. He lifted his rucksack and swung it on to his shoulders then helped Felix with his. "Wait," said Felix and crouched down, pulling Luc with him. He put his finger to his lips and pointed through the trees. Working their way slowly along the path were Joseph and Rita. Felix motioned Luc to crouch down further. Joseph was hunched and Rita held him, one arm at his elbow, the other round his shoulder. He looked older. Felix and Luc watched them pass through the trees looking down all the while until they came to the road that led to the house.

"We need to hurry," whispered Luc. "The bus won't wait for us."

"Another minute," said Felix. "Let them get into the house."

They waited, listening to the wind in the tops of the trees and the waves breaking at the shore. "Let's go," said Luc and they jogged over the undergrowth to the path, to the shore road, to the village where the last passengers were boarding the bus.

Rita led Joseph straight to the bedroom and helped him under the covers then looked for Felix and Luc. Their room was empty. With her coat still on she climbed into the bed beside Joseph.

"They've gone," she said.

"It was time," said Joseph.

When they woke a soft line of early evening light shone between the shutters and Joseph pushed the sheets back to free his arms and chest. "I was standing in a field full of people," he said. "Everyone was clapping. It was terrible."

Rita covered a yawn with her hand. "You were dreaming," she said.

"Then I was in a house at the top of a mountain and I had a headache from running. The rooms in the house were vibrating and filling with sunshine. It was too bright to look at."

"You've slept deeply," said Rita. "I'll make us something to eat."

Joseph closed his eyes. He thought of dressing but he was stuck, a magnet pulling him towards fear and the house was so quiet with the boys gone.

Rita stood at the sink. The window was covered in condensation and she wrote a name with her fingertip, watching the drips from the letters run down the windowpane and collect on the sill. She heard waves beating land and drank, washing away her worries drop by drop until she felt a soothing glow, a memory. She was walking through a forest, soft pink blossom blowing into old apple trees. Their trunks were purple on the windward side and sloping down, healthy but almost scentless.

She took Joseph a glass of water. "It'll help you wake up," she said and sat down beside him and closed her eyes.

Joseph looked at Rita and saw in her face the young woman he first met. He thought of the lagoon on one side, the sea on the other. The thaw was over. Tomorrow they would walk to the shore together. He pictured himself opening the door, but stayed in bed, touching all that he wanted with the soles of his feet.

The Sound

Echo didn't answer the first knock. She was used to kids running through the forest, taking their chances and hammering on the caravan door before disappearing back into the trees, but it was too early for them to be about. The second knock was clear and insistent. Echo put her book face down on the table and pushed the door open. It swung round and snapped into the clasp, and she leaned out over a drenched woman whose hair hung on either side of her high forehead, dripping on to her shoulders.

The woman took a step backwards and put her hands on the bundle tied across her body. Echo looked her up and down. She wore lace-up shoes, grey ankle socks and a dress that clung to her knees. A mewl came from the bundle and a small pink hand stretched out and pawed at the woman's chest.

"Can I come in?" she said.

"Sorry, yes, come in, come in."

Echo stepped aside and let the woman into the caravan. She looked out at the wall of forest, up at the cloudless sky, reached round and pulled the door closed. The woman's teeth were chattering and the baby was making restless squawks. Echo plugged in the heater and waited for the bars to glow. "You're soaking," she said. "Give me your shoes."

The woman prised her heels out without untying the laces and her feet slurped as they freed themselves from the leather. Echo propped the shoes up on their toes against the cupboard in front of the heater to dry. The baby's noises had blended into a low cry now and the woman fumbled at the knot in the makeshift sling.

"I can't untie it," she said. "It's too wet." The cries were getting louder. The woman's hands were shaking as she tried to find some slack in the knot. She looked at Echo for help. "He's hungry." Echo reached into the material tied snugly against the woman's body, gripped the baby round his middle and pulled him out. He was wrapped in a pale blue sweatshirt and she held him away from her while he screamed, his back curling like a hedgehog. Wisps of dark hair covered the curve of his ears.

"I'll take him now."

Echo passed him to the woman who had slipped the cardigan that had held the baby, with its sleeves still knotted together, over her head and unbuttoned her dress to the waist. She sat down on the bench and put the baby to her breast. He fussed a little then drank in gulps while Echo unfolded a blanket and draped it awkwardly round the woman's shoulders.

"I'll make us some tea," said Echo.

Echo glanced back at the woman while she waited for the kettle to boil on the stove. It was hard to tell her age; she was so slight. She looked peaceful enough nursing her baby but the cushion under her would be sodden. Steam spurted from the kettle's spout and Echo filled two mugs, squeezing the teabags between a spoon and her finger. She added milk and slid into the bench opposite.

"I crossed the river," the woman said, without looking up. Echo looked at the baby's head, at the dark hair pressed against its scalp. "I had to hold him above my head at the deepest parts. I was sure we'd drown." Echo pushed the tea towards her. At the estuary the water was wide and even when the tide was out Echo couldn't believe it was shallow enough to cross. If the woman was telling the truth she was lucky she hadn't been swept out to sea.

"What's your name?" said Echo. The woman looked up. Echo wondered if she'd heard her.

"Helle," she said.

"And the baby?"

Helle looked down at the baby as if the thought hadn't occurred to her. "I don't know," she said. "I haven't chosen yet."

From the chest of drawers in the bedroom Echo pulled out trousers rolled up at the ankle and a sweater that had shrunk over the years and sat them on the bench next to Helle. "You'll catch a cold in those wet things. Get yourself changed. You can use the bedroom." The baby had stopped feeding and was asleep in the crook of Helle's arm.

"Do you need to see a doctor?" said Echo. Helle shook her head. "But you'll need things for the baby, nappies and clothes and…" The caravan suddenly felt very full. Echo picked up her book. She'd been trying to identify a lichen she'd seen the day before. The illustration looked like a collapsed tangle of smoke rings. She looked around for something to mark the page then put it back down, splayed open on the table. "Will you be okay here," she said, "if I go to the shop?"

"I'll be fine," said Helle.

Echo rode through the housing on the edge of the town and past the turn-off to the holiday park. She leaned her bike against the wall outside the bank and crossed the road. It was only when she came into town that she was aware of how she looked. Above the sink in the caravan were two lumps of dried glue where a mirror must have been but here she noticed the stares from teenagers and caught her reflection in shop windows, her woollen hat pulled down to her brow and the downturned hem of her overcoat.

The shop had just opened and she stood in front of the nappies and looked for a picture of a baby the size of the one she'd just held. She reached for a pack with a chubby little thing smiling up at a woman's face and put it under her arm then, as an afterthought, took a second. She put them on the counter then went back for a carton of milk, picking up a cherry loaf on her way past. Echo felt her cheeks redden at the till but the boy serving her rang up the goods like any other. What would he care, thought Echo, an old woman buying nappies, hardly the talking point of the town. She put the change in her purse and snapped it shut.

Outside she stuffed the milk in one pocket of her overcoat and the cake in the other then bent to pick up the nappies at her feet. She straightened up and there was Peter.

"Echo?" he said. She hadn't seen him in months. He'd shaved his beard and his skin looked soft and smooth. He said her name again. She could see the flecks of brown in his green eyes and she wanted to answer. For the first time she wanted to speak to him, tell him about the woman and the baby waiting for her in the caravan.

"Sorry," she said and pushed past him, bumping her shoulder against his. The elastic resisted her pull as she tried to fasten the packets on to the back of her bike. "Come on, come on," she said and forced the hook over the bar. She pedalled quickly, forgetting to signal as she swung into the farm road.

The first time she'd seen him after she left had been surprisingly easy. She'd queued behind him in the fishmonger and when he turned to greet her she just looked straight past him, pretending not to know him and, though she detected a slight race in her gut, she kept on looking past him until it felt entirely normal. He bought his fish and when he left the shop she saw the look in his eyes as he walked past. If asked to describe his expression, she could have in the same way she could describe the process of extracting dye from the lichen she collected.

The milk and cake in her pockets swung and bumped against her sides as she pedalled but she was nearly there, just around the corner. Ahead of her a woodpecker swooped above the road flashing its red belly. She pedalled faster, watching it fly then dart between the trees. Something ran in front of her and she heard a noise escape from herself, felt the bike skidding under her weight and landed awkwardly, scuffing her knees and the heel of her hand. She crawled on to the grass verge and watched a cat slip through the hedge on the other side. "Get yourself together woman," she muttered to herself.

It was too quiet. The baby had stopped feeding and Helle sat surrounded by someone else's things. Jars were lined up along the bench, tipped slightly and leaning against the window. At the bottom of each one was a different coloured handful of moss. Condensation had formed on the inside of some of the jars and hung in beads from the glass. She needed some air. She needed to walk to remember. Something was on the tip of her tongue but she couldn't reach it. She tied the baby back around her, closed the door and walked quickly in long strides. The balls of her feet burned against the hard leather soles of her shoes but the sun was warm on her face and she couldn't imagine stopping even if she wanted to.

On either side of the path there were trees. They covered the mounds of sand and moss as far as she could see. Sometimes they creaked and swayed and, where a trunk had broken and fallen, a neighbouring tree had caught it in its branches. Helle tried to remember something, anything, as if piecing together a dream that she'd just woken from. She knew she could do it, that it was just there, if she kept going. Her mouth was dry and she was warmer than she'd ever felt.

What she saw was a group sitting in a circle. She could see the curves of their backs and in the middle, a stool. Two people shuffled apart and a man stepped into the circle carefully lifting a guitar over their heads. He sat on the stool and started strumming. His hair flopped over his face as he looked down at the strings and she could see his mouth moving, but no sound was coming out. She tried again. He stepped over the people in the circle and again he started to play. She couldn't hear his voice. If she recognised the tune, she could sing it to the baby perhaps. The muscles in his forearms twitched as he changed chords and she felt the brush of his arm against hers and they were sitting at a table, just the two of them.

The track was hard and she looked at the slopes of fragile, silver lichen and longed to sink her feet into its spongy surface but at least the path was clear; she could concentrate on remembering and just put one foot in front of the other and it would lead somewhere, back to where she had started, back to the woman who'd given her the clothes, back to the caravan. She remembered that much. The woman had helped her, given her the sweater that clung to her side now where the baby had peed.

She made herself think of the table again and the two of them sitting close together, arms touching. It was how she'd met Glen, she could see him clearly now, the Glen she'd met years before, tanned, healthy and grinning. "You're new here, aren't you?" That's what he'd said to her late that first evening, "You're new here."

The guest house had been full when she arrived in the afternoon but they offered her a spare mattress on the floor in the bunkroom. She'd left her bags and taken a walk through the village. The nearer she'd got to the beach the more sand drifted across the road. She followed the fence round the marina, stopping only to listen to the masts click and hum in the wind, and she climbed the crest of the dune. The wind whipped her hair across her face and she pulled up her hood. The tide was in and she walked across the stones, into the wind, until her face felt numb and she turned to walk the other way following the curve of the coastline into the estuary. On the other side of the sound was a forest and the water that separated them was fast and deep. She turned again into the sheltered cove of the harbour and saw a sign for a cafe.

When she returned to the guest house it was empty. It was too early to go to bed so she sat at the table with a book. When the door opened people crowded in, laughing. They greeted her and busied themselves with filling the kettle and setting out cups for tea and coffee. Glen slid round the bench to sit next to her. His smile was friendly, his voice gentle.

The track was becoming overgrown. If she'd veered off the main path a while back she hadn't noticed. Helle climbed over broken branches, over the dips and tufts of the undergrowth, holding the baby tighter against her as she bent forward, then she climbed one last incline, edged through the trees and the wind caught her. "Breathe," she told herself, "and again. Stand still." She steadied herself on a branch. She remembered following him up the ladder into the loft. Was she that easy? She stood in the dark while he fumbled about looking for matches then lit a candle. She remembered a branch that stood propped by his bed with trinkets hanging from its twigs and a warm pink light under the sheets. She remembered the silhouette of his naked body.

Helle sat down in the coarse grass and peeked in at the baby cradled between her knees and chest. The sudden stillness woke him and while Helle watched him suck on his lips she felt the sting on her breasts then a damp ache as milk spilled out. She looked upstream, to where the riverbank met beaten dunes topped with pine trees that towered over the waves breaking at the river's mouth, then out further, much further, too far to make sense of, to a ship, dark grey on the horizon. The baby cried out and she put him to the breast. He guzzled and she rocked to slow him down. An oystercatcher dipped its orange beak in and out of the silt on the shore next to a tyre stuck fast. How many turns of the tide will it take to release it or will it be buried forever, she wondered.

The ground felt damp and she shifted to one side but realised it was her that was wet. She tilted her body and ran her hand under her leg. The trousers were sodden and the palm of her hand was smeared red. The boat sheds on the other side of the river were painted in different pastel shades. Out front there were figures moving, dancing maybe. She thought she could hear strumming. She watched the flow of the water, waiting for a seal to break the surface. It was definitely music. She shut her eyes and listened to the overlapping wind and water, the peep-peep of the oystercatcher and picked out the faint gusts of a tune.

The radio was crackling and flicking between stations so Peter turned it off and listened to the cough of the engine instead. Smoke rose from the hills where farmers were burning heather. It was the first time Echo had looked at him, really looked at him since she left. He'd caught her off guard, he knew that, but to see a crack in the glaze she'd perfected so swiftly after she left made his heart quicken and offered him hope — hope for what he wasn't sure, but when he drove home he sat in the car outside the house they'd built together unable to get out.

She'd started to speak to him. She'd stopped herself but that didn't matter now: she'd started and that was all that was important. But what on earth was she doing buying nappies? He reversed over the cattle grid, turned in the track where it dipped down to the chicken coops and drove back through the village to the turn-off that led to the edge of the forest.

As long as they'd known each other, Echo had gone walking by herself once a year, sometimes twice. It had never bothered Peter. He managed just fine on his own. She'd check the weather forecast and if it was dry she'd pack a small bag and set off for a night, two at the most. If she planned the direction she was heading in, she didn't say and when she returned she slipped back into their routine as if she hadn't been away. It was always the same until three years ago. Peter had waited and waited and when the weather turned bad he phoned the police. It wasn't that he was worried about her, he'd tried to explain to the officer, Echo could look after herself. "Did he want them to look for her?" the officer asked.

"Yes, I want you to look for her." But Peter knew she wasn't coming back. He searched for a word to describe how he felt, a name for the weight in his shoulders and legs. It was sadness, spreading through every inch of his body as he realised the distance that had grown between them. The police officer returned later that day. He'd asked around and she was staying in a caravan near the farm at the edge of the forest. Did Peter want him to speak to her, he wanted to know.

"No, leave her," said Peter. "She wants to be alone."

Peter wanted to invite the young man in, tell him about the weeks of silence before she left, how she'd gone from talking only when necessary to not at all, but instead he stood in the threshold of their house and watched him drive away.

The figure sitting at the side of the road was instantly recognisable. Echo was hunched on the grass rubbing her knee. Her bike lay beside her with its front wheel pointing skyward and her hat had fallen off. Her thick hair, cut short at the nape of her neck, was greyer than the last time he'd seen it. Peter pulled over and Echo stared at him as he got out of the car.

"Are you following me?" she said.

"I wanted to see if you were all right," Peter said, standing well back.

"Well I am," she said. "You can go now." She waved her hand, brushing him away like a ball of dust.

"Echo," he said, crouching down, "are you sure?" She pulled her trouser leg from her boot, spat on her grazed knee, yanked up a fistful of grass and rubbed it on the wound.

"You can go back into the town if you want to,"

she said without looking at him, "get me some baby clothes."

"Baby clothes?"

She stood up and grabbed her bike. "Do you want to help or not?"

"I do."

"Try the charity shops then. A sleepsuit, anything." And she cycled off. Peter picked up her hat from the road and shook the gravel from between the stitches. He wondered if he should follow her, find out more, but he got the impression that to turn up empty-handed would be the wrong thing to do.

He drove back to town and parked by the seafront. A sleepsuit. He tried to picture what that was. An all-in-one kind of garment, he imagined, that poppered down the front much like the long johns he'd taken to wearing in the winter months under his overalls. There were three or four charity shops on the high street. He went into the first one. The racks of clothes were grouped into similar colours.

"Baby things?" Peter asked at the counter.

The woman pointed to the back of the shop, to a pile of plastic toys and a stack of dog-eared books. "There's just a few bits and pieces," she said.

"Any clothes?" asked Peter.

"We don't get much in," said the woman. "People want new things these days." She took a plastic bag from a smartly dressed woman. "There's a shop two doors down. You'll find what you need there."

Peter stood in front of the window looking at the frills, the coordinating prams and outfits displayed in the window. He didn't know how many times he must have walked up and down this street and he'd never noticed this shop. He started to open the door then shut it again. He'd try another charity shop first. He headed straight for the back this time and on a rack hung a few small dresses, a raincoat and between them a job lot of terry towelling sleepsuits: pale blue, pink and yellow. He didn't know if the baby was a boy or a girl. He didn't know anything about the baby for that matter or if there was even a baby at all. He picked up the yellow sleepsuits and took them to the counter.

Echo opened the door. No one was there. What were you expecting, she thought to herself, for her not to move the whole time you were gone? But then she saw the dress lying in a soggy heap on the floor in front of the blazing heater. Echo turned the heater off, wrung the dress out over the sink and shook it back to shape. Over the pattern of small green squares ran washed-out streaks of what looked like blood and scattered round the hem were rusty flecks. Still holding it, she ran into the clearing and shouted "Helle. Helle, are you there?" It was strange hearing her voice so loudly when days could pass so easily without her speaking to anyone. "Helle, I've got things for the baby," she yelled.

Echo pegged the dress on the line tied between the caravan and the nearest tree where it hung limp next to the rags Echo had dyed to tear up and weave. Something fell at her feet. It was an envelope folded in half. Echo prised it open but the ink had all but disappeared. It was thick in the middle where a letter must have been but to remove it would destroy it. She put it in her pocket. She stood in the clearing and shouted the woman's name again then stood still, waiting for a reply. She had no idea which direction she would have gone in. All Echo had lost was a pair old of cords and a jumper and she told herself Helle would be fine, that she could manage but, when she heard the familiar sound behind her, Echo ran towards Peter's ancient car.

"She's gone," said Echo before Peter could shut the door. "She said she'd walked across the river. It's impossible isn't it?"

"Hold on, hold on," said Peter. "You need to slow down."

"The baby's so young, I don't know if there's time." She grabbed her hat out of Peter's hands, pulled it on and started walking into the forest. "We need to find her," she called back. Peter jogged along the track trying to keep up with her.

Glen listened to the clatter of bowls in the sink, the rustle of the cereal packet and the fridge door slamming shut. "I'll be through in a minute," he said into his pillow. He hoped the kid had thought to rinse the bowl out before eating from it. He heard footsteps coming closer but drifted back to sleep. When he opened his eyes he saw Alex sitting on the edge of the mattress spooning cereal into his mouth. He worked his arm out from under the blankets and put his hand on the boy's bare leg. It was freezing.

"How long have you been sitting there?"

"Not long," said Alex and he tipped the bowl to

show the dregs of milk and cornflakes at the bottom. Glen rolled over and reached for his phone to check the time.

"Jesus, Alex, it's too early. Climb in for a bit." Glen lifted the covers for Alex to get in then turned his back towards him. He felt the child's bony knees against the back of his legs.

"Will we look today, Dad?"

Glen turned over and brushed the boy's hair down with his hand. "We'll look today." He watched his eyes close and his breaths become shallow. Would he look? He didn't know. He didn't know if Helle even wanted to be found and how could he explain that to the boy?

Glen woke again with a start. He checked his watch and looked at Alex sleeping soundly, his mouth slightly open. He shook his shoulder. "Alex." He shook him harder. "Alex. Wake up." The boy opened his eyes and stared up at him. "We've slept in. You need to get to school." Alex was about to say something. "I'll look while you're there," said Glen. He sat up, put his feet on the floorboards and when the boy's arms started to reach round his waist, he stood up. "Come on kid, let's get moving." They dressed from the piles of clothes on the floor and grabbed their coats from beside the front door.

Glen stood at the end of the lane and watched Alex run. "Go straight to the main door," he called after him. Alex stopped. He hitched his bag up on his shoulders.

"Promise you'll look?" he shouted.

"Go on," Glen waved him up the path. "You're

late." He waited until Alex turned the corner, banging his bag against the hedge, then walked back down the shore road, stopping at the gate to hook the word "No" in front of the "Vacancies" sign that Helle had painted on a piece of board she'd found washed up on the beach. There had been hardly any guests in the last few months, and the long-term rents had packed up and moved on, starting with Marie. She had been there from the beginning and, once Marie left, word got around.

The paint on the front of the house was wind beaten and peeling, and plaster fell to the floor as Glen shut the door that had swelled and no longer fit in its frame. He sat at the table and rolled a cigarette. Tobacco spilled on to its scratched surface and the spidery threads mixed with crumbs and stuck to spilt milk.

Guests used to gather round the table in the evening to eat and talk. Helle would put a big pot in the centre with a serving spoon and a stack of mismatched dishes before sitting down to join them. When they finished Glen helped clear up then played his guitar. That was when it was going well. Glen tapped ash on to the floor. He took his phone from his back pocket and scrolled through the numbers but there was no one to phone. He had no idea where Helle would go. Their life revolved around this house and the people that came and left it but none of that mattered now; the baby was due in three weeks, maybe less.

When Helle first came to him she brought very little: a couple of bags of clothes, an old camera case filled with notebooks, and a tube of rolled-up photographs. She'd wanted to arrange an exhibition in the town, teach classes locally, but it was summer and the guest house was busy; he needed her help. Then Alex was born. He remembered one morning, Helle coming downstairs with Alex on her shoulder, her eyes dark from lack of sleep. He was washing the breakfast dishes and whistling.

"You're happy," she said.

"I know. I was just chatting with Marie about the plans for the new art centre. She's on the committee. You should speak to her."

"She doesn't like me," said Helle, switching Alex to the other shoulder.

"Of course she likes you."

"She doesn't," said Helle. "I speak to her and she stares at me like I'm talking nonsense."

"She's listening."

"But she doesn't answer, she doesn't tell me what she thinks." Helle rubbed Alex's back.

"She's valuing what you say, giving you her time."

"I don't want to be given her time. I'm not looking for her approval." Alex hiccupped and spewed undigested milk down her back. Helle grabbed the dish towel from Glen and tried to reach over her shoulder to wipe the sick.

"She's a good listener," he said.

"And I'm not?" she snapped.

Glen knew that whatever he said would be wrong. Since Alex was born if they weren't rushing past each other to get the jobs done around the house Helle was feeding Alex for hours on end. Helle handed Alex to him while she cleaned herself up and put away the cups on the shelf.

"You're going to break those," he said.
"I want her to move out," said Helle.
"What?"
"Marie, I want her to move out."
"She can't," said Glen, "she's been here longer than us."
"She'll find somewhere else." Helle took Alex back and went upstairs. "Unless you'd rather I went," she shouted from the landing.

Marie worked in the cafe at the harbour. Glen looked forward to her coming home at the end of the day; in the morning, when he looked down the shore road and caught the flick of her turquoise coat as she turned the corner towards the harbour, he longed to follow it. Helle had reason to be jealous, he knew that, but he also knew that Marie was out of reach, she'd made that clear. When he started working at the guest house he'd go along to the cafe when he knew it'd be quiet and Marie would stop what she was doing for a chat. He thought there was something between them, a meeting of minds or simply lust, but when he sat down with his coffee he saw her eyes rest on every customer in the same way.

Glen heated up a cup of coffee in the microwave and buttered a crust of bread. As he leaned back against the cupboards and ate he noticed Helle's poster tube on top of the kitchen units. He stood on a chair and lifted it down. It was covered in a sticky film of dust and he took a damp cloth, wiped it clean then wiped the table, sweeping all the crumbs and scraps into his hand and putting them in the bin. He dried the table then unscrewed the case and pulled out the roll of photographs. He separated them and spread them out on the table around him, weighting down the curled corners with books. Each photograph was different. One was a blast of yellow that was almost too bright to look at; another pink, red and orange like a tropical sunset; another purple and blue like a satin cushion. The last one was almost black but with slashes of colour bursting through like light through a heavy curtain. Why had she never shown him these? Had he never asked? He remembered her telling him about how she made them. He rolled the photos up on his knee and slid them back into the case. He should shower, he thought. Then he would start looking.

Helle wiped her hand on the grass. The tide was going out. The water glistened and the boats bobbed near the harbour but, at its deepest point, the pull of the current churned the water in opposite directions. She looked again at the building divided in three by different colours: blue, yellow, terracotta — the cafe, the shop and the boat shed.

She'd spent two nights with Glen that first time, that was all. During the day she'd wandered round the village and sat on the beach while he worked until they met again in the evening. He told her his plans: the couple that owned the guest house were leaving, going travelling, they were going to leave him in charge but he didn't think they would come back. He had plans for the place and was going to offer to buy it from them. He had enough saved for the deposit, he told her. She told him her plans to study photography.

At the bus stop he held her as she cried into his T-shirt. It was the end of summer and her body ached from their nights together. He waved her off, blew kisses and the bus left the village. Helle took the last roll of film from her pocket, put her hands deep into her rucksack and edged out a length of film. She pulled the drawstring tight, clipped the bag shut and put it on the seat next to her with her arm round it. She sat back and watched the fields and villages pass.

After two days of buses, boats and train journeys she arrived at her parents' house. Helle went straight to her bathroom where she kept the chemicals. She pulled the curtain over the window above the door and, before she turned out the light, she set out the spool, the scissors and the canister on the shelf and memorised their positions. In the dark she pulled out the entire length of film and fed it on to the spool, twisting it in alternate directions until it was wound on. Then she dropped the spool into the canister, screwed in the funnel and turned on the light.

She printed while she waited. Each film she'd exposed on the journey turned out a different colour depending on the amount of light that had reached it through the layers of clothes. While she developed the photos she thought about Glen and why they had taken the risks they had. She couldn't call it love. They'd spent such a short time together and she knew nothing about him. He belonged wholly to that house, the village and those two days and, anyway, looking for answers was pointless because her period was late.

She did a test and laid it next to bottles of developer, fixer and stop until two blue lines appeared. There was no mistaking it. Helle sat down at her desk, opened the window on to the late summer afternoon and wrote Glen a letter.

At first she counted the days it would take for her letter to reach Glen and the days it would take for a letter to come back. Then she counted again, giving him a day to reply, then a day to think and another to reply. She was due to start her course at university; she needed to know. When a letter did come back the envelope was thin. There was one page. He wasn't sure how he felt, he was in shock, but she should come.

How long had she been sitting there, remembering so clearly a time years ago when it was the last few days she was trying to grasp hold of? The sound was a ribbon of water separating her from the other side; now the tide was out and she was cold. She peeked in at the baby and he raised his eyebrows into the wrinkles on his forehead and yawned.

She hadn't kept that letter from Glen, hadn't even read it a second time. He'd said to come and that was exactly what she'd wanted to hear but, so often since then, she'd wondered if he'd meant it. Maybe she'd moved to be with him on the slightest shred of evidence that he wanted her there. Maybe it didn't matter; so much had happened. But the morning she left him it was all she could think of and, though she needed to go, get out in the open, something stopped her. She had to at least try to explain.

Glen had hurried out with Alex early that morning, leaving the table covered with bills and receipts. Piles of papers set to topple. She edged a sheet of paper out from between two books. It was smooth and clean. Helle started writing but each sentence she wrote she scored out, unsure if what she was saying was true. Everything she started to say took her back to the beginning but she had to keep going. She wrote in circles, circles that overlapped then closed around each other, until the whole sheet was full. She found another. She needed to tell Glen why she had to go, why she had to leave him. And Alex.

Helle's throat filled with something. She swallowed and let out a sob. She tried to catch her breath but her shoulders heaved and tears fell on the baby. Focus on Alex, she told herself, Alex running, his blonde hair tangled from sleep, Alex who never stood still. And the sheets of paper she'd filled with attempts to explain.

She remembered scribbling through her words, the pen nib scoring across the grain of the wooden tabletop then trailing along the walls as she ran upstairs to look for more paper. Helle shut her eyes. The paper was huge, the size of a house. She blinked it away.

She took the baby from the sling. He was sound asleep. His hand flopped to his side when she lifted it. She wrapped him tightly, nestled him into the grass, took off her clothes and folded them in a pile beside him. Her thighs were smeared with blood. She walked down to the shore where the sand was soft, moulding round her feet with each step.

Echo heard a cry over the wind. "Listen," she said. Peter stopped walking and they stood still. It was coming from close by. Echo followed the wails that stopped then started again, each time louder than before, until she reached the crest of the dune and the bundle at her feet. "Shh now, come here," Echo said, scooping the baby up from the long grass. She felt his cheek with the back of her hand. "He's cold, where is she?"

"Look," said Peter, pointing towards the river. Helle was walking out of the water with her arms folded against her chest. Peter ran down to the shore, pulled his coat off and threw it around her shivering body.

"I needed to wash," said Helle. Her teeth were chattering. Peter put his arm around her and walked her up to where Echo waited with the baby snug against her shoulder.

"Come out of the wind," said Echo. "What were you thinking?"

"I'm sorry," said Helle, "your clothes…"

Echo picked up the stained trousers. "They'll wash," she said, "but put them back on, for God's sake, before you freeze." Echo put her finger in the baby's mouth to stop him crying. She felt his gums rooting against her skin. Helle crouched to tie her shoes. Her fingers were mottled from the cold and she fumbled with the laces. It seemed to take forever and Echo wanted to help but she was holding the baby. They needed to get into the warmth of the forest.

"Thank you," said Helle, reaching out for the baby. "I remembered something. The baby's father." She pointed across the water. "It's the blue house," she said. "His name's Glen. Can you find him and tell him?"

"I'll go on ahead," said Peter, "take the car and see if I can." Echo nodded and he headed off into the forest.

"It's quite a walk back to the caravan, Helle. Do you think you can manage?" said Echo.

"I'm okay. A little light-headed but okay."

"Let me carry him then." Echo took the baby and tucked him under her coat. They climbed over uneven ground and on to the track. "Just tell me when you need to stop," she said. Dappled sunlight covered the forest floor and they walked. When the baby wriggled against her, Echo shifted her grip on him. "Helle," she said, "when was he born?"

"I'm trying to piece it together," said Helle.

"But you remember crossing the river?"

"The river?"

"You told me this morning."

"Did I? But it's too deep isn't it?"

"You said you held him above your head."

Helle laughed. "I couldn't have, could I?" she said.

The road out of the village had been quiet the morning she left but when it met the main road the pavement ended and she stood with her back to the hedge when she heard a car coming. It stopped. The driver wound down the window and offered her a lift. Helle got in. She recognised the woman but couldn't place her. The woman seemed to know her though and she was full of questions: where was Helle going, was Alex looking forward to the new baby? She wanted to answer but her sentences broke off. She asked the woman to stop the car. "What here?" the woman said. Yes, here. Pine trees lined the road. Helle remembered the quiet once the car had turned the corner and disappeared.

She looked at Echo holding the baby under her coat. "I had a bag," she said.

"What?"

"I had a bag when I left. I wanted to go out on the sandbar, see the wild flowers. It's the right time of year for them. I couldn't remember how."

"It's hard to get out there if you don't know the way," said Echo.

"I used to know the way," said Helle. The baby squawked under Echo's coat. "I'll take him now."

The bag had grown heavy, banging against her leg. She would leave it, come back for it later. Looking around she saw a tree with a knot like a cat's eye and sat her bag between its roots. She needed to be moving. If she walked far enough maybe everything would become clear and she could go home but, for now, it was like looking back into the mouth of a tunnel. The best thing was to keep going.

She ignored the pains at first, they didn't last long, didn't cause her to break her stride but then something ripped inside her and she doubled up on the ground. She crawled off the path. If she just lay down for a while … but it came again. She heard panting, imagined the loose tongue of a dog beside her then realised the sound belonged to her. She crawled some more until she found a trough in the dunes where the crust of the earth had broken and slumped into a hollow. A layer of pine needles covered the sand and she curled into the pain when it came. In the distance, waves washed over stones as the tide pulled back then rolled in and she breathed in time until the pains joined together and flooded her.

"I think I had him here," said Helle

"Here?"

"In the forest — he was born here."

The baby was screaming now.

"Let's sit down," said Echo. "You can feed him."

They sat on a fallen trunk and Helle hitched up her jumper to feed the baby. They both stared ahead and said nothing for a while. The longer they were quiet, the louder the birdsong grew in the trees that surrounded them.

"Was that your husband?" said Helle.

"Peter? We never married."

"He's kind."

"He'll find Glen for you."

"And Alex?"

"Alex?"

"My son, he's nearly seven."

Echo rubbed her hair under her hat. She thought about the milk and cake she'd left on the step of the caravan and wished she'd brought it along.

Peter waited for the traffic lights to change. There were roadworks on the way into the village. He hadn't been this way in a while. The extra miles around the estuary put him off and he could get all he needed closer to home. On the other side of the river he could see the dunes where they'd found Helle. They looked steeper from here and the trees looked impenetrable. It was hard to imagine the web of paths behind them. The lights turned green.

He couldn't see the house she'd described. All the houses were whitewashed or pebble-dashed. It must be further round the headland. He followed the one-way system through the village past the handful of shops and the single-screen cinema until the road turned right and back along the shore. There it was. He stopped the car. The paint was faded and peeling, hanging in strips as if the house had been clawed at.

Peter rang the doorbell and waited. He rang it again then knocked on the door harder than he meant to. He heard someone coming. The man who opened it wore a parka and work boots. Round his left eye the skin was yellow and purple and slightly swollen. He rubbed it self-consciously.

"Glen?" said Peter.

"Can I help you?"

"My name's Peter," he said and offered his hand to shake. Glen put his hands in his pockets.

"We've found Helle. That is, my wife found her. And the baby."

Glen stepped out on to the doorstep. "The baby?"

"Yes," said Peter. "The baby."

"But it's too early. It isn't due…"

"Well it's here, a little boy."

Glen steadied himself on the door frame.

"I'll give you a lift, take you to them, if you like."

Glen closed the front door and sat on the bench under the window. He held his head in his hands.

"I don't know if she'll want me."

"She's asking for you."

Peter sat down next to Glen. He leaned forward to be level with him. "She doesn't seem well," Peter said. "I mean, she's fine, the baby's fine. She doesn't want doctors, but she's confused."

"Where did she have the baby? Was she with your wife?"

"I don't know. I don't think so. Don't you..." Peter stopped.

"She left a week ago," said Glen. "I don't know where she's been staying. She told me not to come looking for her. I thought she'd come back. For Alex."

When they reached the caravan Helle followed Echo to the bedroom. "Get some sleep and I'll make you something to eat," said Echo. She stood at the foot of the bed for a second then pulled the door behind her. Helle lay down on her side with her knees pulled up and her arm over the baby. She pulled the blanket from the bottom of the bed up over her legs and patted it round them both. She remembered shivering, lying curled like this and looking up at the sky shining through the treetops with the baby new and naked on her chest. The pain had been everything but she'd pushed him out, held him and waited for the afterbirth. She tore a strip of cotton from her hem and tied it tightly round the cord and when it stopped pulsing she bit through it and buried the purple sack under handfuls of moss. She must have fallen asleep because when she woke up she was trembling with cold. She lifted her head and put her hand on the baby's back to check it was breathing. They couldn't keep lying like this. They needed to move.

As she walked over the moss to find the path blood dripped from her, leaving rust-coloured spots on the silvery green lichen. "I have to get clean," whispered Helle to the baby. She walked to the shore. The waves were noisy, breaking against the pebbles and whipping up a line of brown foam. She went to lay the baby down but the wind was cold and sand whipped against her ankles. She took her shoes off, hung her coat over a piece of driftwood and walked into the water with the baby in her arms. The water was icy but the sting against her flesh dulled the throb in her groin. Helle walked as deep as her chest, her skirt floated up around her and she held the baby high in the air and ducked under the water, counting until her breath ran out. She came out, her head buzzing from the cold, and smiled down at the baby. "Let's get out of here," she said.

Echo tapped an egg on the side of the jug, cracked the shell open with her thumbs and watched the yolk split and bleed into the white as it hit the bottom. She'd prepare the omelette now but let Helle sleep for a while, as long as she needed to. She could cook it when she woke. Echo cracked two more eggs in, whisked them with a drop of water and went outside to cut some herbs from the patch she'd dug next to the caravan. With Helle and the baby asleep, every movement she made seemed louder than usual, the fork hitting the side of the jug, her footsteps on the creaking floor and the knock in the pipes when she ran the tap. She closed the door quietly behind her, relieved to be out in the open where the sounds of bird call masked her own. She took scissors from her pocket and cut a bunch of chervil, inhaling the aniseed scent that the cut released. As strange as it was to have someone encroach on her space it felt good to be doing something for someone other than herself. There was a necessity to what she was doing and she felt more awake than she had for as long as she could remember, but there was still part of her that wanted to push it away, sink back into the undisturbed existence she'd known that morning. She sat down on a rock.

The way she'd left Peter was a choice; she knew that but she couldn't pinpoint the time, the moment she'd made the decision. She'd gone walking much like she'd gone many times before, without packing any more or any less. She'd headed east along the coast, following the disused railway track that cut into the cliffs, dipping down into rocky bays then, when she approached a town, she headed inland across fields and woodland until the light began to fade and she looked for a sheltered place to sleep. She used these times alone not to think but to clear her mind. Other people sat still to achieve this; Echo needed to keep moving. For the first hours thoughts and concerns about the details of her daily life would rush through her head like oncoming traffic and she let them pass trying not to get caught on any one thing until all she noticed was the sounds around her and her own breathing. She walked in different seasons and in different directions and every time on the first, sometimes the second morning after she'd woken with the birds, boiled water for tea and eaten some bread, she found herself leaning towards home. She never walked back the way she'd come; instead she curved her route and circled back towards the land that Peter had found. This last time it was colder than before and she'd shivered all through the night. The sheet of canvas she'd propped up with branches did little to shelter her from the wind but in the morning she kept walking east, resisting the pull of a warm house. It was only the outskirts of a city that made her back up and head along the coast.

Four nights she spent sleeping out in the coldest weather she'd known for the time of year and on the fifth when snow began to fall in the late afternoon she called in on a farm and asked if they had somewhere she could sleep for the night. The way the farmer looked at her reminded her what she must look like and he looked back at the fire blazing in his kitchen and the evening meal spread out on the table. His wife came to the door pulling her oven gloves off and flicking them over her shoulder. Did she want to come in, have some food with them? "No," said Echo. All she wanted was somewhere for the night, maybe longer. "I can pay," she said.

The farmer put his boots on and she followed him across the yard and over a field to the edge of the forest. He pointed into the trees. "There's an old caravan in there," he said. "You're welcome to it."

Echo nodded and he went on through the trees to a clearing. The caravan was streaked in rust and dirt, and moss was growing at its joints and when the farmer opened the door it smelt damp, but there was a bed and a stove and the roof was sound. "It's fine," said Echo. The farmer shrugged as if it didn't matter either way to him what she did. "I'll bring a plate over," he said. "Steak pie, it'll warm you up." "Thank you," said Echo.

The sun had moved behind the trees and the rock was in the shade. Echo stood and touched Helle's dress round the collar and hem where the material was thickest. It was dry and she took it off the line. She felt for the letter she'd found: it was still damp and compressed but she put it back in the dress pocket. In the distance she thought she heard the drum roll of a woodpecker. She stopped to listen but it didn't come again. The chervil. That was what she'd come out for. She picked up the bunch from the rock and went back inside. She was hungry herself now. She'd cook the omelette and if the smell didn't wake Helle she would heat it up later.

Glen stared out of the window while Peter drove the car. He caught a bit of what Peter was saying about it being none of his business but to feel free if he wanted to talk. "Thanks, I'm okay," said Glen. He had been relieved when Helle left. He was exhausted but he needed to clean the place before Alex came home from school. He filled a bucket with warm, soapy water, threw a sponge into it and carried it upstairs. The first marks were on the stairwell and he rubbed at them but the pen had scored deep into the wallpaper. As he climbed the stairs the marks formed a line that looped back on itself and started to form a pattern but he knew the tangle it led to. She had got hold of Alex's felt-tip pens, and behind the upturned chests of drawers, the wardrobes fallen against the beds, the walls were covered from floor to ceiling in scrawls and scribbles. Glen dropped the sponge back in the bucket and closed the doors. There didn't seem any point in even starting. He brought bedding down to the small sitting room off the kitchen. They would sleep there for now.

For weeks they had been going round in circles, over and over the same thing. Helle wanted Marie to leave but Glen wouldn't ask her. She had become like a dog chasing its tail, on and on, forgetting why she had started in the first place. All reason had gone but no one had the energy to stop. He tried to imagine Helle in the rooms — where had she found the strength to push over the furniture? — but all he remembered was coming home. He'd dropped Alex at school then gone to the supermarket to pick up cleaning stuff and food for the next couple of days. When he opened the front door Helle was there as if she'd been waiting for him. Her face was flushed, her eyes wide and the buttons on her dress had burst open across her stomach. Before he could say anything he fell back, dropping the bags and clutching at his face. He moved his hands to see if she was coming for him again but she stood perfectly still, staring back at him, then picked up the holdall at her feet and pushed past him. He watched her walk down the road that led out of the village. He didn't try to stop her.

Beyond the brown blankets and beige walls Helle could see the tips of trees and the cloudless blue sky. She'd slept soundly with the baby tucked in at her side. The skin on his eyelids flickered. What could he be dreaming of at such a young age? She touched his head and then his chest ever so gently so as not to wake him but to feel the life in him. She wanted Glen to see him. He looked different to Alex when he was born: he was slighter, his features more angular. He looked more like her. Her face was heart-shaped, Glen had told her, and he pretended to draw on her face, starting on her high forehead, following the hairline round her ears that she thought stuck out too much, then down to the point of her chin and up the other side.

The cushion was damp under Helle's cheek. She hadn't noticed she was crying. She would never have come back to Glen if it hadn't been for Alex growing inside her. But how could she know that? She hadn't struggled over a decision. Once she knew she was pregnant and once she knew Glen wanted her to come, she came. What else could she have done? Not had the baby? The thought didn't cross her mind. Begin her studies and try and juggle motherhood with student life? Again it wasn't something that needed any thought. And the final option to stay in her parents' house was not something she was willing to consider even for a moment. No, the baby's father wanted her to come and when she thought of their nights together she felt a warm tug in her stomach. It was pleasure and it was pain but it was proof to Helle that her feelings were strong enough to travel to be with him, so she had barely unpacked and she was packing again. She took clothes, her notebooks and a roll of photographs made over the summer.

The day she arrived back in the village was still and overcast. The bus dropped her on the shore road and she walked down to the house. The door was slightly ajar. Through the gap Helle saw Glen sitting at the table next to a woman, their heads bent towards each other. She knocked.

"Helle," he said, pushing his chair back and taking the bag from her shoulder. "Why didn't you phone?" On the dresser next to the door was a pile of letters with a postcard on top. She picked up the picture of her hometown.

"I sent you this."

"It must have come this morning," he said, lifting the pile from the dresser and sifting through it. He put the letters down. "Sorry," he said. He leaned towards her then hesitated, put his hands on her shoulders and kissed her on the cheek. "Can I get you anything?" He started filling the kettle, "A cup of tea?"

The woman at the table cleared her throat. Helle recognised her from before, from the cafe. Her hair was greying at the roots but henna-red curls fell around her face and down her back. Helle remembered talking to her one day while she was waiting to meet Glen. They talked about nothing in particular — the weather, travelling — but she was friendly and Helle, buoyant from the night before, had welcomed the conversation.

"This is Marie," said Glen.

"We've met," said Helle. Marie looked like she was trying to place her, like she recognised her but wasn't sure from where. "At the cafe," said Helle.

"I know," said Marie, "I remember." She folded her arms and leaned on the table. "Will you be staying with us longer this time?" she said.

Helle looked at Glen. She waited for him to say something, to turn the moment into anything other than what it was. He said nothing. She felt her throat clench and her eyes smart but she smiled at Marie and went to stand next to Glen at the sink.

"I'll be here for a while," she said.

"Good," said Marie, standing up. She pulled her coat from the back of the chair and slung it over her arm. "We'll have time to get to know each other then." She looked from Helle to Glen, smiled and closed the door behind her.

Peter's car pulled up and Echo turned off the gas, slid the frying pan to the back of the hob and went out to meet them.

"You must be Glen," she said.

"That's right," said Glen. "Are they okay?"

"They're sleeping," said Echo, "but come in."

Glen followed Echo into the caravan and waited while she took a plate from the cupboard and sliced the omelette with a spatula. "Are you hungry?" she said.

"I'm fine," said Glen.

"Well, take this in with you." Echo handed the plate to Glen and opened the door to the bedroom where Helle was awake and sitting up. "Glen's here," said Echo, standing sideways to let him in, "call me if you need anything."

"Thank you," said Helle.

Echo split the rest of the omelette between two plates and went back outside to where Peter was leaning against the bonnet of the car. "Here," she said, "you must be hungry." She led Peter to the bench she'd made at the end of the van by balancing a plank of wood on two stacks of bricks. They sat down next to one another, ate without speaking, then put the plates on the bench between them.

"That was good, thank you," said Peter.

"It's been a long morning," said Echo.

"It certainly has." Peter stretched his legs out in front of him. He scratched his head.

Echo thought to ask about the farm, how Peter was managing. She knew the struggle it must be to carry the workload they had divided over the years. He must hate her for leaving him without warning, with everything they had built together to look after. To ask would be insulting. Peter had rested his head against the caravan and shut his eyes. Echo looked at the soft folds of skin where his beard used to be. She imagined reaching out and touching his cheek but kept her hands in her lap. "Did you find him easily enough?" she said.

Peter opened his eyes and nodded. "Fairly," he said. He bent to tie his bootlaces that had come loose.

"Their house is in some state by the looks of things."

"But he seems okay?" said Echo. "I mean, we're doing the right thing aren't we, bringing them together?" Echo thought of the bruising round Glen's eye. It was a few days old at least but it looked painful.

"I think so. He was keen to come." Peter got up and walked to the washing line. He fingered the ribbons of cotton that hung like washed-up seaweed. "I thought I'd take them to the farm," he said. "I'll suggest it."

"Really?" said Echo.

"They can stay while they work things out. Glen can do some work for me in the meantime."

Glen sat on the edge of the bed and put his hand on the baby's chest, barely touching him but enough to feel the rise and fall of his chest. "Can I hold him?" he said. Helle nodded. Glen slid his arm under the baby's back and lifted him. The baby yawned, his eyebrows trembling with the effort.

"Can you dress him? Echo left some clothes." Helle pointed to the end of the bed and Glen reached for the nappy, vest and yellow towelling sleepsuit folded in a little pile.

"Come on then, let's get you decent," said Glen and he lay the baby on his back, lifted his feet and fastened a nappy round his stomach.

"Fold it down," said Helle, "so it doesn't bump the cord."

"I know," said Glen. "I'll give it a clean too."

"Don't. He's too sleepy. Just dress him for now."

Glen pulled the vest over his head and put his

hands and feet into the suit then fastened him up. The baby stirred, made noises as if to cry then settled again.

"Have you given him a name?"

"No, not yet."

"How about Farlan?"

"Where did that come from?"

"I remember hearing it on the radio." Glen looked at the baby fast asleep with his hands above his head.

"Maybe. Farlan. I need to get used to it," said Helle and she shut her eyes.

"I have to go and get Alex from school," said Glen.

"He'll be glad it's a boy," said Helle.

Glen nodded. "Helle," he said, "are you okay? Are you sure you don't need to see a doctor, get the baby checked?"

She swept the hair away from Glen's forehead touched his brow then his cheek. "I'm sorry," said Helle.

Glen took Helle's hand and held it on his knee. "It's okay," he said.

Peter waited in the car while Glen stood at the bottom of the lane and when the school bell rang the children ran down in a tangle of bags and coats. Glen saw Alex walking slowly, letting the faster children bump past him. He waved but Alex didn't smile and when he reached Glen he dropped his bag to the ground. Glen smoothed down his thick blonde hair. "We've found your mum," he said.

"Really?"

"We're going to see her now." Glen picked up Alex's bag. "And you've got a brother, Farlan."

"Yes!" Alex punched the air. "What's he like?"

"Well, he's like a baby. You'll see." Peter was waiting by the car. "This is Alex. Alex, this is Peter. He found your mum."

"Pleased to meet you," said Peter, extending a hand for the boy to shake.

"Alex stay here with Peter and I'll run into the house to grab a few things."

"Why?"

"We might be staying with Peter for a while."

"But I want to pack my things."

"You stay here, okay? It'll be quicker."

Glen unlocked the front door and ran up the stairs. Glen remembered the day Helle's letter arrived. The house was full of guests, there were breakfasts to make, bedding to change, cleaning to be done. She had written her address on the back of the envelope. He put it in his pocket to read later and in the lull in the afternoon between old guests leaving and new ones arriving Glen went down to the rocky seafront, rolled a cigarette and opened the letter. The paper was written on both sides. He could hardly keep up with what Helle was saying: she was staying with her parents, she missed travelling, spending time in her room, printing photographs and she was pregnant. They knew there had been a possibility. He walked along the rocks to the cafe.

It was quiet and Marie untied her apron, folded it under the counter then walked with Glen past the boat shed and along the bay. They sat in the grass with the windsock falling and rising above them, a rope rattling against the pole.

"It'll mean the end of us," said Glen.

Marie took his hands in hers. "There isn't really an 'us' though, is there?" she said. She patted his hands and looked out over the water. "She's right for you. If she wasn't you wouldn't have let this happen." Was that why he'd let this happen? He wasn't sure. It was too late to think about that now anyway.

"Do you want me to clear off?" said Marie. "I'll find somewhere else."

"No," said Glen. "I want you to stay."

Marie looked at him, testing him. "Now don't you be thinking you can have it all," she said with a laugh.

"I won't," said Glen.

Marie patted his hand. "I need to get back," she said.

They walked back along the shore and Glen reached for Marie one last time. She pulled her hand away and he caught it again. She gave it a squeeze. "That's it now," she said and looked him in the eye. "You're going to be a daddy, Glen. If you can't do that with me around then say, okay?"

Glen stood on the waterfront smoking a cigarette. He turned back once and saw Marie laughing with the younger waitresses, tossing her head back then leaning in for a conspiratorial whisper. She smoothed the apron across her stomach and as she tied the strings at her back she caught his eye and winked. Would she stay, he wondered. He couldn't imagine the place without her.

He took a holdall from under the bed, shook the dust off it and stuffed in some of his and Helle's clothes. He stopped at the door on the landing halfway up the stairs. He pushed it open. The room had lain empty since Marie had moved out. Guests wanted the upstairs rooms or the loft, not this one on the stairwell where they might be disturbed by footsteps on the stairs. Glen thought about the number of times he had wanted to knock on the door as he passed it on his way to bed knowing that Helle would be asleep but not knowing if he'd be invited in or not. He lifted the mattress and propped it up against the wall. The pink and orange throw Marie had pinned up in place of a headboard had been ripped from the drawing pins that fastened it to the wall and lay in pieces, scattered across the room like rose petals.

Nobody spoke as they drove to Peter's house: through the town, past the turn-off to Echo's caravan, then inland along a winding road. Peter took the bends without thinking then slowed to turn on to the steep track that led to his land. The ruts on the track were worn and he drove to one side to stop them from getting deeper.

"Are we there yet?" said Alex.

"Nearly," said Peter. They slowed down and rattled over a cattle grid. A tractor stood in the middle of the field next to the track, its trailer tipped towards the ground. "That was one of today's jobs," said Peter, "picking up stones from the field. Maybe you can help me later, Alex. He looked in the rear-view mirror. Alex was looking back at him. You just walk behind and throw the stones into the trailer." Alex didn't answer. "Or maybe you'd like to ride up in the tractor with me?" Alex grinned. "We'll see once your mum's here." He turned into the driveway. "Here we are." An old collie ran to greet them. "That's Lexie," said Peter. "Don't go after her, she'll come to you if she wants to."

Glen and Alex got out of the car and stood in the driveway looking around at the greenhouse, the chicken coops. "Look," said Alex pointing at a tree house on the other side of the field.

"I built that," said Peter, "for children who come here on holiday."

"Can I play on it?"

"On you go." Peter looked at Glen. "If that's all right with your dad. The stile's further along there." He pointed down the track. "And go wide round the sheep, they're getting ready to lamb."

"Thanks Peter," said Glen.

"It's fine." Peter lifted the bag out of the boot of the car. "Let me show you where things are. I've some things to take care of before I go and fetch Helle."

Glen made a cup of tea and took it outside. He could see Alex peeking out the window of the tree house. He was shouting something and Glen waved. Peter came out of the house and joined him. "Some place you've got here," said Glen. They watched Alex climb down from the tree house, pick something up from the ground and climb up again.

"Echo and I came here years ago. We'd been looking for land and this valley was for sale. We had big plans…" Peter trailed off.

"So she doesn't live here now?" said Glen.

"No, she doesn't." They sipped their tea and watched Alex running across the field towards them. "Which means," said Peter, his voice upbeat, "there's too much for me to do alone." He looked at Glen, "If you need work I mean."

Glen scuffed his feet in the gravel.

"I don't mean to interfere," Peter went on, "but the offer's there. We'd be helping each other out." Peter put his hand on Glen's shoulder. "I'll go and get Helle shall I? And the baby."

"We're going to call him Farlan."

Peter opened the car door. "Farlan," he said, "I like it." He drove out of the driveway and rolled down the window. "I'm going to get your mum and your brother," he shouted to Alex on the other side of the fence. "You can show them round when I get back." He waved and drove down the track.

With Glen gone, the baby dressed and food in her stomach Helle felt stronger. She sat at the table and watched Echo at the sink. "Peter's taken Glen to fetch Alex," Echo said. "He's going to take them to his house then come back for you."

"I don't want to go back."

"You don't have to, Peter has space; you can stay there for as long as you need to."

"I don't think I ever want to go back," said Helle.

Echo dried the plates with a dish towel and stacked them back in the cupboard. "You need to rest Helle. Can I get you anything else?"

The cherry loaf was still in its wrapper on the table. "A piece of that maybe," said Helle. "I'm starving suddenly."

"That's good," said Echo. "That's a good sign."
"A sign of what?"
"That you're feeling better, getting stronger."
Echo sat down with Helle and opened the cake.
"Do you like living out here, all on your own?" said Helle.
Echo stopped. She looked at Helle. "I get on fine," she said.
"But what do you do?"
"I fill my time," she said. "I collect lichen from the forest and I use the dyes for my rugs."
"You don't get lonely?"
"Not lonely, no."
"But Peter…"
"You ask a lot of questions," said Echo.

Glen drained the last of his tea, put his cup on the front doorstep and went to meet Alex who was climbing back over the stile.
"Did you see me Dad?" he was shouting.
"I did, I saw you."
"D'you want to come back with me, I'll show you how to climb up? There are bits of wood nailed to the trunk to help you get up."
"Maybe later, Alex, why don't we explore down this way?" Glen pointed down the track they'd come along. "Down to the loch then we can cut across that field and be back for your mum."
"Okay," said Alex. He was disappointed, Glen thought, but they could climb the tree later. He wanted to have a look at the place. Glen eased the bolt on the gate and the chickens ran to them. He

opened it just enough for Alex to slip through.

"Quickly now," he said, "better not let them out." And he shut the gate behind him. Alex scurried behind Glen, tripping over heels. "You're not scared are you?" said Glen.

"No," said Alex holding on to the back of Glen's coat.

"They think we're going to feed them," said Glen. "Come on." They climbed over the next gate and the path turned into deep tractor tracks. "Stick to the highest bits and you'll not get too muddy," said Glen and they kept on the smooth crusts of mud until they came to a digger mangled up in the short stubby trees.

"Is it broken, Dad?" said Alex.

"I don't think so," said Glen. "Peter said he was clearing some of the land for holiday cabins. Maybe he meant here."

"Look."

Behind a mound of grit lay an upturned rowing boat with scratches scored into its fibreglass hull as if it had been dragged along the ground. Its oars stuck out from underneath.

"Can we go in it?" said Alex. "Please."

"Not just now, Alex." Glen crouched down beside Alex. "We'll have plenty of time for all these things," he said. "We're going to be staying here for a while."

"What about school?"

"I'll take you, don't worry."

"What about the house?"

Glen stood up. He threw a stone far into the water and picked up another. Alex picked up a handful and started throwing them in one after the other. "I think it's time for a change." He looked at the boy who was gathering as many stones as he could carry. "That all right with you?"

"That's all right with me."

"Good," said Glen. He found a flat stone and skimmed it out over the water. "Seven bounces, Alex, did you see that?" But Alex was running round the shore, jumping between tussocks of grass. "Wait for me," called Glen.

Peter opened the car door for Helle. She hesitated. "I don't have a seat for the baby," she said.

"I didn't think of that," said Peter.

Helle climbed in and pulled the seat belt over herself and Farlan.

"I'll drive carefully," said Peter. He shut the door and looked at Echo.

"I'm not coming with you," she said.

"Come for a while," said Peter. "I can always bring you back."

Echo thought about the road up to the house, the gorse bushes that lined the track up the hill that would be coming into flower and their sweet coconut scent that the wind carried uphill. She thought of the window she'd painted in the workshop and the colours that splashed into the room on a bright day and the warmth of the eggs she picked up every morning from under the straw. If she went back now she didn't know if she could leave again and she needed time to think. "You go on for now. I've done all I can to help."

"But the baby?"

"The baby's fine. They can stay with you for a while can't they?"

"Of course, there's plenty of space if they want it. Glen can help out. It's up to them."

Helle wound down the window. "Thank you," she said.

"Good luck," said Echo.

"Will you come and see us?" said Helle.

Echo nodded. "I'll try. I've some things to do here," she said, "but I'd like to. I'd like to meet Alex."

Echo waited until the car had gone then went back into the caravan. She picked up the book she'd been reading that morning and sat down at the table. It had been left face down for so long she doubted the spine would recover. She looked at the black-and-white diagram again of lichen tissue. Earlier it had reminded her of a congested coastline with roads, railway tracks and tunnels crossing over one another, jostling for space. Looking again she saw the cells born from the tangle, the inevitability of expansion. She closed the book round her finger. The baby was so small, so new. She could still smell his warm milky breath from when she held him while Helle got into the car. He'd snuffled and slurped at her neck, looking for his mother's milk. Her baby had never breathed, not one intake. The midwife had wrapped him in a blanket even though the cold didn't matter to him now and handed him to Peter. Peter rocked him and cried. He held him to his chest then lowered him to Echo. She turned to the wall. "Take him away," she'd said. "Take him away."

Echo threw down the book and ran out of the caravan. She started towards the trees but they were full of everything that had happened that day. She ran back into the van, into the bedroom. The blue sweatshirt lay on the rumpled bedcovers. Echo grabbed it. She pulled a bag from under the bed and stuffed it in then took some clothes from the drawers and pushed them in on top. At the sink she filled a bottle with water, put the rest of the cake in the bag and left the caravan. She walked along the side of the road until she was lost in the rhythm of her strides. It would be light until late that evening and then she would sleep. In the morning she would make a fire, drink some tea and decide which direction to walk in.

The Nest

Alice stood behind the curtain watching Edna play on the veranda. It was too hot out there, even in the shade. Edna was holding a doll in each hand, moving them and mouthing words Alice couldn't hear. The swing seat had stopped creaking and the maid was asleep with Edna's mango in her lap. Its sweet smell hung in the humid air. The maid's head rolled forward and her arm fell to her side, her hand still gripping the knife. As she exhaled her fingers loosened until they opened and the knife hit the tiles. Edna jumped. The maid rubbed her nose with her hand, but her eyes stayed closed.

"What are you doing?" said Alice from the doorway.

"Shh, you'll wake her."

"She's meant to be looking after us." Alice picked up the knife. "How long has she been asleep?"

"I don't know," said Edna.

"You must know."

"I was playing."

Alice ran her finger along the blade, wiping it clean of the fruit's flesh. "Go and get supplies," she said, "and meet me in the hideout."

"Why?"

"Just go," said Alice. "I'll keep watch."

Edna set her dolls down, stood up very slowly and tiptoed towards the door. The maid grunted and Edna froze, balanced on the ball of her foot, looking at Alice who mouthed her to keep going. She waited until the maid's breathing turned to shallow puffs then she ran past Alice and into the living room. The house was cool and dark inside. Edna blinked to adjust her eyes.

She crept past the mahogany staircase that led to the bedrooms and along the passage to the kitchen, avoiding the Persian runners that skidded on the polished floor. She wondered where Isaac was. He'd been watering the garden earlier. He'd soaked her ankle socks and she'd laughed because it meant she could take off the socks and sandals that their mother insisted they wore and go barefoot instead. She hadn't seen him since.

The store cupboard was at the end of the passage, just before the kitchen and opposite the dining room. The large door was painted pale blue to match the floral oilcloth stuck to the shelves. Edna could see what she was after. She reached as high as she could and nudged the old Nescafé jar with her fingertips until it fell towards her and she caught it in both hands. They were in luck. It had been restocked with the boudoir biscuits that she and Alice loved to suck until the sponge disintegrated on their tongues, leaving a trace of sugar and stale coffee. Edna put the jar in her pinafore pocket and peered into the kitchen.

A pot was simmering on the back of the stove, filling the air with the smell of boiled cabbage, and the back door was open. She could slip out that way and round the back of the house but she would have to pass the outhouse, where the maid and Isaac lived, and the Alsatian that pulled and snarled on the chain pegged into the ground. She padded back up the passage and crossed the hallway. The front door was sitting open, letting a cool breeze in. Her mother would never have allowed that. She could go that way but from the living room she would be able to see the porch swing and check if the maid was still asleep.

Edna stopped before she went into the room. She hugged the door frame and peeked round until she could see the French doors. The swing seat was still and there was Alice, next to the maid, bending over her. She was holding something at the maid's neck. Edna took a step into the room, then another. Sunlight glinted off the knife in Alice's hand. Edna squealed and ran.

She ran out of the front door and across the lawn, jumping over the hosepipe that trickled into the grass, past the squares of banana trees, heading for the hideout by the tennis court. Footsteps followed her but she didn't dare look back as she ran through the pineapple grove and down the embankment of red earth to the hole she and Alice had dug under the pine trees. Edna threw herself down on the hard soil and covered her eyes while the footsteps got closer and closer. She felt a thud on the ground next to her and moved a finger to one side. It was Alice.

"How are we going to bury her?" said Edna between breaths.

"What?"

"How are we going to bury her? She's huge. We can't dig a hole big enough. It's taken us long enough to dig this out." Edna pointed at the curve of dug out soil they were sitting in, at the roots that poked through the red earth and tickled the backs of their necks.

"She's not dead, stupid," said Alice.

"How do you know?" Edna felt like crying. She also

felt like peeing and concentrated hard on preventing both.

"I wanted to see what colour their blood is," said Alice.

"Maggie's?"

"Magdalena. Her name is Magdalena."

"She told me to call her Maggie," said Edna. "What colour is it?"

"I didn't get to find out, did I, with you squealing like a little pig?"

"Where is the knife?" said Edna.

"I dropped it."

Edna let out a whimper and a stream of urine ran down the slope. "They're going to come after us," she said. "They're going to kill us." Alice put her arm around Edna's shoulder.

The knife had been so perfectly sharp, like the razors wrapped in greaseproof paper their father kept in his bathroom cabinet. Its point was like a needle and when Alice pressed it into the fleshy tip of her index finger the mound of skin turned white around it. Magdalena's breathing had been steady. She was as big as a mountain and Alice wondered how the chains that held the chair didn't break. She expected her to snore but instead she purred like an old lioness and her bosom rose and fell like the swell of a wave while a vein pulsed at the curve of her collar bone. Alice very gently placed the tip of the knife on the bulge of the vein and watched the skin rise around it with each breath. She pressed down on it, just a little, just enough for the skin to pale and stretch then pressed again, a little harder. Her own breathing slowed and fell in time with Magdalena's. Her hand started to tremble. The skin would surely break soon. She leaned forward until she could smell the sweat on the maid's blouse then a scream came from inside the house. Magdalena woke up. Alice remembered the creamy whites of her eyes, the pitch black of the pupils that stared straight at her. Then she was running.

Edna pulled her knickers off, rolled them into a ball, tucked them into a gap under a root and covered them in loose earth. Her fingernails were clogged with dirt. "Look," she said and held her hands out, palms down, for Alice to see. "We're not allowed to get this dirty." She wiped her runny nose and the dirt smeared across her cheek.

"Hold still," said Alice and she spat on Edna's hands. "Now rub them together." Edna rubbed her hands until they were coated in a soupy mixture of spit, sweat and earth.

"How long are we going to stay here?" she said.

"I don't know," said Alice. "I really don't know."

Their mother's shoulders were all bones and hollows and she held her head at the same angle as their father. Alice had noticed this travelling home from school the week before. From the back seat she watched as they turned to one another to speak then looked ahead, their heads tilting to one side. It was the end of term. While the girls hugged their friends, their father put the trunks in the boot then waited in the car for the girls to climb in the back. Within minutes of setting off, their legs were sticking to the leather seats. They'd been travelling some time when their mother stretched her pale slender arm behind their father and turned to speak to them. "Your father and I are going on a trip, isn't that exciting?"

Alice scowled.

"Will Flora look after us?" said Edna.

"No," said their mother keeping her smile bright and easy, "not Flora, Magdalena."

"Who's Magdalena?" said Edna.

"And where's Flora?" said Alice.

The girls had grown up with Flora. There was a photograph Alice liked to look at of herself as a toddler strapped on to Flora's back and Edna, a newborn, strapped on to her front. She imagined Flora toppling if either one of them were taken off.

"She stole from us, didn't she?" Their mother turned to their father, who nodded. "The tiger's eye bracelet your father gave me, you know the one. So we sent her away. The new maid will look after you. She's a better cook than Flora, don't you think?" Their mother looked for their father's agreement again but it didn't come. When they pulled up outside the house the new maid was waiting for them.

"She looks like a statue," said Alice.

"Don't be impertinent," their mother said and waved. The new maid didn't wave back. She kept her hands clasped together over her thick waist.

"See?" said Alice. "A statue." Edna giggled and as soon as they were out of the car she ran for the garden but Magdalena caught her by the sleeve.

"Out of your uniforms, girls, before you play," said their mother, adjusting her skirt around her hips.

"And freshen up. Such a long journey." She fanned a glove in front of her face. The maid put her hands on the girls' backs, led them into the house and up to the bathroom where she pulled a stool across the tiles for Edna to stand at the sink.

"You're our new Flora," said Edna, rubbing the soap between her hands. Alice dug her elbow into her side. "She's our new Flora," said Edna. "What's wrong with that?"

"Nobody can be a new anybody," said Alice. Edna looked at the froth on her fingers and ran them under the tap.

"My name is Magdalena," said Magdalena, holding a towel. Edna stepped off the stool to dry her hands and Alice took her turn.

"Magdalena," whispered Edna. The syllables rolled off her tongue. She tried it again. "I like it," she said.

From the hideout they could see the gate beyond the hedge draped in bougainvillea. It was open. It was always open. Alice often wondered what the point was of having such a heavy iron gate, with such a sturdy bolt on it, if you never shut it. They liked to swing on the gate and wait for cars to pass but they never went further. "White girls don't walk," their mother had said last summer when Alice suggested they stroll down the hill to the sea. Instead they piled their bathing suits and towels into straw bags and climbed into the car.

"Do you remember the trip to the beach?" said Alice. Edna nodded though the memory was confused with a story someone at school had told her about a missing dog whose owner lost it one night while walking on the cliffs. They went on looking until it was too dark to continue and the next day the dog was found, washed up on the sand below. "Do you remember Edna? Daddy was away and we begged and begged for Mummy to take us until she gave in."

It was near the end of the holidays and such a hot day. "At least there'll be a breeze at the sea," their mother had said when she'd finally agreed. "But I don't want you telling your father I took you." Alice remembered it clearly.

As soon as they set off their mother became excited. She stopped the car at the side of the road where a woman was selling guavas. "I want you to taste these," their mother said and, with a knife from the picnic basket, she cut the fruit in half and passed them back to the girls then tightened her headscarf under her chin, rolled the windows down and turned the radio up full volume. She sang along as they wound round the coastal road with the girls sucking on the fruit in the back seat. Alice scraped out all the seeds with her tongue and threw the shell out the window. As the car swung round a bend she watched it bounce off rocky outcrops as it fell. She started to feel sick. She leaned forward and shouted over the music and the wind.

"Will we be there soon?"

"Not long now," their mother called back over her shoulder. "I'm trying to remember a bay your father took me to years ago. It's somewhere along here." Alice sat back. From the house they could have been at the water's edge in half an hour.

"Do you think she knows where she's going?" said Edna. Alice shrugged then, without warning, the car swerved off the road and came to a sudden stop. Their mother got out of the car, slammed the door and ran to look. She whisked off her headscarf and shook her hair loose in the wind, then ran back and leaned through the window.

"This is it," she said. "I knew I'd find it." She opened the door. "Come on."

Edna took the picnic rug from the back shelf and Alice carried the basket that had sat between them. They followed their mother through the long grass. The path was narrow and steep. Their mother stumbled and laughed. "I don't remember it being this wild," she said. "Quite an adventure, isn't it, girls?" Edna held on to the grass and tried not to slide. Alice tucked the basket under her arm to keep the other one free in case she fell. Below them she saw a sandy beach and crisp turquoise water.

They stopped where the path ended and stood on the rocks looking over the bay. On the far side of the beach was a group of figures, silhouetted against the pale yellow sand. "Oh," said their mother. "I thought we might have the place to ourselves." She looked back up the path. Alice put the basket down. "Never mind, it's a family. Look. We'll stay over here and we'll be just fine." She jumped from the rock on to the sand and reached up to carry Edna down, then took the basket from Alice. Edna dropped the rug on the sand and they shook it out, sat down and unpacked the basket. Their mother poured lemonade into cups she'd had Flora wrap in tea towels and they drank while they watched the other family drag a boat down to the shore.

"Are they going fishing?" said Alice.

"I don't know, dear. Try not to stare, Edna."

"Can we go and play?" said Edna. "Did you bring our bathing suits?"

"I didn't. Tuck your skirts in your knicker elastics if you have to." They ran towards the water. "And girls," their mother called, "stay on this side of the bay."

The sand felt hot on their feet and Alice held Edna's hand and made her run until they reached the wet sand and the water washed over their toes. They jumped over the waves and watched their footprints vanish. The boat was coming in their direction pulled by a boy waist-deep in the water.

"What are they doing?" said Edna.

"Don't look at them."

"He's waving," said Edna.

"Don't wave back," said Alice. Edna waved. The boat was level with them and the boy stopped.

"Do you want a turn?" he said.

"No," said Alice.

"Are you scared?"

Alice looked back at the rug. Their mother was lying down, using the basket as a pillow. Her ankles were crossed but her hands were by her side. Alice guessed she was sleeping.

"I'll have a turn," said Edna.

"You can't," said Alice.

"I won't let go," said the boy.

The two children in the boat were younger than

Edna, little more than babies, their hair braided into knots that covered their heads. Edna was walking out towards them. Alice grabbed her arm. "We'll get in trouble," she said.

"I don't care," said Edna.

The boy pulled the boat to meet her. His shorts clung to his legs. "Climb in," he said.

"Edna, please," said Alice.

The boat rocked as Edna pulled herself over the side and the children giggled. The boy pushed them into deeper water until the waves lapped under his arms.

"Not too far," shouted Alice.

She ran along the shore as the boy pushed the boat. The waves rolled in and the boat slid over them. As they neared the other end of the bay Alice noticed the white-topped waves further out. The wind was picking up. "Watch out," she shouted. A wave bumped the boat, sending a spray over Edna and the babies, who yelped as the water hit their skin. The waves were getting bigger. The boy turned the boat and started towards the shore. Alice looked beyond him. A swell was rising. Edna saw the wave and leaned over the side, paddling with her hands but it crested, caught the stern and the boat tipped on its side, pouring the children into the sea. Alice screamed. She saw the boy fish the babies out, one then the other. He held them, crying, under his arms and, before she could move, somebody dived past her into the shallow water and scooped out Edna, who came up coughing and spluttering.

"Alice!" their mother shouted. She was running up

the beach, her headscarf flowing from her hand. She stopped at the water's edge, looked at the man holding her soaking daughter, looked at Alice, raised her hand and slapped Alice on the cheek.

The man stood Edna down and their mother grabbed her hand and pulled her across the sand with Alice running behind them. The sand pushed Alice's feet outwards. She thought of the way she'd seen ballerinas run on to the stage. I'll walk like this from now on, she thought. I'll tell the girls at school it's from spending all summer on the beach. Their mother snatched up the rug and the basket and climbed up the hill faster than Alice had ever seen her move. Edna scrambled after her. Alice stopped to look back at the bay, at the family huddled together on the far rocks. The boy stood and waved.

In the car Edna sat snivelling in the back, wrapped in the picnic rug. Their mother put the radio on then turned it off again and they drove in silence. The only word their mother spoke to them was once they were back in the driveway. She opened the car doors, pulled the girls out, looked down at them with her lips pursed together and shook her head. "Bed," she said and pointed to the house.

The sun was high in the sky and the branches overhead did little to protect them from the midday heat. "Alice, do you think you might have killed her, without realising it?" said Edna.

"I don't think so."

"Why aren't they looking for us then?"

"They don't really care about us. It's their job to look after us, that's all."

"But won't they get in trouble with Daddy if they lose us?"

"They know we're not lost. How could we get lost in our own garden?"

"I suppose," said Edna. "But we've been away a long time." She dusted the film of earth on her shins. "I'm getting hungry." Alice unscrewed the lid of the jar and pulled out four biscuits, gave two to Edna and put the lid back on.

"We won't eat them all now. We don't know how long we're going to be out here."

Edna sucked on the biscuit, comforted by the sugar on her tongue. "I should have taken some milk. I forgot," said Edna with her mouth full.

Between the girls and the tennis court was a pile of stones. Every year stonemasons came to build another wall "to stop the house sliding down the hill", their father joked.

"It's for privacy," their mother said. "We don't want people peering into our lives do we now?"

"Don't you want to see out?" Edna asked and their mother laughed.

"We have everything here and we want to keep it to ourselves." She pulled Edna on to her knee. "It's only natural. You'll see when you're older and you have your own house. Now run along and play."

At dinner their parents talked about the new fences their neighbours were putting up. From the car Alice had seen razor wire curling along the top of walls and shards of glass set in a layer of concrete spread along the walls like icing. The old lady that lived across the street had been burgled but luckily, her father said, she was in the habit of keeping a baseball bat and a handbell next to the bed. The servants had woken to her ringing and rushed into the house before anything could be stolen. Their father had a gun in a display case in his study and bullets in his desk drawer and he talked about installing a security gate but their mother laughed and said, "We have Isaac's dog. That thing would rip any intruder to shreds before he got near the house."

Edna put her head on Alice's stomach. "I'm going to sleep," she said. Alice's insides gurgled and Edna closed her eyes and let her head be lifted by her sister's breathing. Alice took the hair clip that hung on a strand of Edna's hair, stroked down her fringe and clipped it back in. She put her arm behind her head, shut her eyes and listened to the crickets chirrup in the branches above. As her lids grew heavy she thought how careful she'd been, pressing the blade on the vein. She didn't want to make a cut, just a pinprick that would let out a trickle she could catch on her handkerchief. Alice heard her name being called from far away. She tried to answer but her lips were dry and stuck together. They kept calling but, as hard as she tried to prise them apart, no sound would come out.

"Alice, Alice, wake up." Someone was shaking her knee. She opened her eyes and saw Magdalena stand upright and block out the sun. Edna stood beside her with her filthy underwear clenched in one hand.

Magdalena took Edna's hand and started walking up to the house and Alice followed them, brushing the earth from her skirt. She thought of the cool lemonade her mother served in a jug with ice cubes and a long stirring spoon as she followed them through the French doors and into the living room.

"Sit down," said Magdalena pointing to the sofa. Alice looked at her skirt, red with earth, and Edna's, which was even dirtier. "Sit down," Magdalena said again. They sat on the very edge of the cream cushions with their hands in their laps while Magdalena pulled up a chair. The rattan seat was fraying at the corners and Alice wondered if it would hold her weight and if their mother had allowed her to use this room. Flora would never have entered the living room without permission or instruction.

"There's been an accident," Magdalena started.

"What kind of accident?" said Edna.

"Our parents?" said Alice.

"That's right," said Magdalena.

"Are they dead?" said Edna.

Magdalena said nothing.

Edna fell against Alice, sobbing into her shoulder. Magdalena heaved herself off the chair and left the room. Isaac was in the garden. He was leaning against his rake and picking at a tooth far back in his mouth and watching them. He shook his head very slowly back and forth then started raking the lawn, stopping only to pull off the dried leaves that caught on the prongs.

"What happened, Alice?" said Edna.

"I don't know. A car crash, maybe."

There was a girl at school, Alice couldn't remember her name, but she remembered her being called out of class one day and never coming back. Her desk was cleared and her locker in the dorm emptied. The story had gone round that her parents had been killed in a car crash on their way to visit her and she had been sent to live on a farm with her grandparents. Alice felt a tear run down her cheek and hunched her shoulder to wipe it away. She pulled Edna towards her and tried to comfort her.

The French doors framed the garden. It was so vibrant and lush compared to the room they sat in. A pattern of faded damask roses trailed over the cream sofa and armchairs — their mother's choice. Along one wall was a bookcase with a set of encyclopedias bound in burgundy leather that Alice had never seen her parents look at. On their mother's bureau were photos of their parents on their wedding day, photos of their grandparents and christening photos of Edna and Alice, taken two years apart but identical behind the frills of lace.

Their mother entertained in this room. Alice and Edna would sneak down to watch ladies perch on the edge of the sofa, balance teacups on saucers and exchange gossip about their maids and their neighbours. Sometimes they sipped from high glasses and sucked olives from cocktail sticks. It was then that Alice and Edna might be called into the room and their mother would pull them to her side, smooth their dresses and tell her friends how clever Alice was, how well she was doing at school. She would wrap one of Edna's curls round her finger and let it drop. "This one is the pretty one, of course," she would say. Alice looked at herself in the mirror later and wondered if she was doing well at school because she wasn't pretty or if her looks were being hindered by her intelligence. She rubbed at her slim cheeks until they glowed red and practised smiling with her lips shut to hide her grown-up teeth that seemed too large for her face.

Alice looked at the dust that had fallen from their clothes on to the furniture. She tried to rub it off but it became embedded in the weave of the cloth. "Let's go upstairs," she said, "to the balcony."

The balcony was a room nestled into the eaves that housed furniture which was too old and worn for the rest of the house. There were, amongst other things, two daybeds, foldaway garden chairs and a wobbly desk; the girls liked to sleep out there on hot nights though Edna was scared of the geckos that climbed the walls and stuck to the ceiling. They tried to decide what they were more scared of, their transparent skin or the possibility of the geckos losing their grip and falling on them while they slept. Edna would giggle with fear and hide under the covers. They pulled over two chairs, leaned their elbows on the ledge and looked down into the garden. Magdalena and Isaac where talking by the birdbath.

"What's going to happen?" said Edna.

"Let's wait and see," said Alice.

She thought of her mother and father in the front seat of their car. She imagined them talking, arguing even and driving faster and faster as their voices grew louder. What had they been arguing about? Alice remembered the sharp corners on the coast road that had turned her stomach and she pictured the car screeching off the road, falling and turning until it crashed in a heap on the rocks below. Or had they been driving so fast that the car sped from the road and nosedived into the sea? Magdalena had told them nothing, she realised. Maybe they had stopped in a town for lunch, had been crossing the road to a restaurant when a truck filled with crates of fruit ran a red light and hit them both head-on.

Isaac looked up at them and laughed. He reminded Alice of a snake, the way his eyes narrowed and his skin was wrinkled like old leather, but Edna said he was kind. The first time Alice came back from boarding school Edna told her how she'd found a bird flapping in the red dust under the pine trees and Isaac had helped her look after it.

"Tell me again about the bird you found," said Alice.

"What?" said Edna, wiping her nose on the hem of her skirt.

"The bird you rescued from the dirt."

Edna smiled as she remembered the colour on its head and wings: blue like the jewels on their mother's necklace. Its beak was broad and long. She'd crouched down and watched it, waiting to see if it would lift itself into the air and fly back to its nest but it stumbled and flapped until it gave up and just lay in the settling dust. Very slowly Edna had crept towards the bird: she knew not to frighten it. She scooped it up and its wings fluttered against her palms. It tickled but she kept her hands closed gently round the bird and carried it back to the house. Isaac was watering the borders on the driveway and he put down the hose when he saw her coming with her hands held out in front of her. "What have you got there?" he said.

"A kingfisher," said Edna. She recognised the bird from the frieze that ran round the walls of her classroom at infant school. "K is for kingfisher," the class would chant when the teacher pointed to the picture of the bird that looked so grand and strong compared to the fragile thing lying in her hands.

"Let me see," said Isaac. He bent down and Edna moved her thumbs just enough for him to make out the bird. The light agitated it and it scrabbled to get free. Its claws scratched her skin and she thought she might drop it. "Let me take it," said Isaac. Edna looked at him. She wasn't sure if she could trust him.

"I want to look after it," she said.

"You will," said Isaac. "I'll help you." He placed his hand over the bird so that its head slotted between his forefinger and middle finger. The rest of his fingers wrapped around each wing. "Got it," he said.

Edna followed him to the shed at the side of the house. With his free hand Isaac took a bunch of keys from his pocket, shuffled them through his fingers until he found the right one and unlocked the padlock. The door was stiff and Isaac kicked it loose. Inside it smelled of damp earth and wood. Garden tools leaned against the walls of the shed and old paint pots were balanced in leaning stacks. A lawnmower had fallen and lay across the doorway and

Isaac stepped across it to the worktable at the back. He took a cardboard box from a shelf and tipped out the contents. A door handle, some screws and a dried-up bottle of glue rolled across the table. "This box is good," he said. He looked around the shed still holding the bird. "There," he said, "give me that cloth."

Edna climbed over the lawnmower into the shed. Cobwebs caught in her hair and she brushed them away, pretending not to be scared. She saw the cloth he was pointing to: an old towelling square wrapped around an oilcan. She unwound it and handed it to Isaac, who shook it out and draped it over the box. "The bird will stay here," he said, sliding his hand under the cloth.

"What will it eat?" said Edna.

Edna followed Isaac back to the house and waited in the drive while he went into the outhouse. He came out with a jam jar lid, an open can of dog food and a bowl. She watched as he dripped some water from the hose into the lid and carried it to the shed. He put it on the ground while he scraped chunks of jellied meat into the bowl, breaking them up with a fork. "This will make it strong," said Isaac. He put the food and water in the box with the bird and left the shed door ajar. "It needs to be quiet," he said.

Every day when she came home from school she went with Isaac and gave the bird clean water and fresh food. Edna worried. "It's so dark in there," she said. "Won't it be cold?" But Isaac repeated, "It needs to be quiet." Then one day Isaac picked up the box and brought it outside. He carried it down to the earthy slope where Edna had found it and put the box on the ground.

"Let's see if it can fly," he said.

He lifted the cloth from the box and the bird splayed its wings. It scrabbled around on the smooth base of the box; Isaac gently tipped the box and it slid on to the ground. It flapped its wings against the dust. "Come on," said Edna. Isaac put his finger to his lips. The bird hopped. It spread its wings, took off and was gone in a streak of colour.

There was a knock on the door frame. Edna jumped off her chair and stood next to Alice. Magdalena was behind them with a cloth looped through her apron strings. "Come and help me in the kitchen," she said. "It's time to eat." The girls followed her downstairs.

"Will I set the table?" said Alice, pausing at the dining room. The mahogany table was uncovered and still had, as its centrepiece, the silver fruit bowl they weren't allowed to touch, though the fruit sometimes turned blue and furry on its underside.

"No," said Magdalena, "you'll eat with us." They went into the kitchen and Magdalena opened the drawer next to the sink. She handed Alice a knife. "You know how to use this, I think." Alice felt her cheeks burn. Magdalena took a cabbage from the cupboard and put it on the board. "Shred this," she said. She gave Edna a bowl of sugar snap peas. "You can shell these," she said.

The girls stood side by side and did what they were told while Magdalena stirred mealie pap in a pot on the stove. She had her own stove outside and Alice wondered why she didn't just use that, then she wouldn't have to carry the pot so far. When she'd finished chopping the cabbage Magdalena lifted the board and scraped it into a pot of boiling water then poured in the peas. "Wait outside," she said.

"Outside?" said Edna.

"Outside," said Magdalena.

Isaac was already lying on the hard ground at the back of the house. He was chewing on something and throwing scraps to the dog, who snapped and scratched at the flakes of dried meat that landed out of its reach.

Edna looked at Alice to see what she should do and Alice sat on the ground so Edna did the same. Magdalena brought out the pot and put it down, kicking Isaac's leg on the way past. He went into their rooms and brought out metal bowls. He scooped out the pap, passed them to the girls and Magdalena ladled the vegetables on top. Alice waited to see how they were going to eat without cutlery. Isaac and Magdalena rolled the pap around in their fingers. Edna copied. Alice tried a little. It tasted like the stewed dumplings they had at school. She was hungry and finished the bowl before Edna. Magdalena took their plates, her face impossible to read.

They put themselves to bed that night. It didn't feel so different. Their mother read to them when she was in a good mood but most nights she mixed herself a drink and shooed them away saying, "Alice will tell you a story."

The stories began with princesses with long flowing hair and horses that could speak, things Alice knew Edna would like, but something bad always happened that made the princess scared and unhappy, and Edna would climb into Alice's bed to listen to how the princess became a normal little girl who wished she had older brothers and got in trouble no matter how good she was. By the time Alice reached the end of the story Edna was asleep. They would start again the next night. But that night Alice didn't want to make anything up. She was too busy thinking about where they were going to live and who was going to come and collect them.

"Do the teachers stay at school in the holidays?" said Edna.

"They go home like us," said Alice. "I thought you were asleep."

"Do they live far away?"

"They live near the school."

"So, they don't live in the school?"

"No, only the housemistress does."

"And she lives there all the time, doesn't she?"

"When we're there, yes, but she has her own home too."

"Why?"

"So she can have her own family and her own things."

"What things?"

"You know, furniture, ornaments, her own maid. Why are you asking all this?"

"I was thinking it might be easiest to stay at school. In the holidays, I mean. But if there's no one to look after us…"

"There's no one to look after us," said Alice. She leaned over and turned off the light but she couldn't shut her eyes. Alice thought back to the fuss that was made about her starting at the new school. There had been fittings for her uniform, the new trunk with the heavy lock she kept catching her fingers in. Games with Edna were sombre rehearsals for their separation. They fashioned uniforms for their dolls from tissue paper and made them say goodbye to each other over and over again. Sometimes they would pretend to weep as they waved the dolls' plastic hands; sometimes they would make the dolls embrace and tell each other how much they would miss each other; sometimes they pretended that they'd never liked each other anyway and that they were glad to be rid of each other. However the dolls behaved, the game ended in Alice reassuring Edna that she would be back in the holidays and that, in just two years, she too would be going to school and they would be leaving together.

When it came time for Alice to go, their father took time off work. The plan was for them all to drive north, spend an hour or two at the school settling Alice in then they would leave to get home before dark. "No point in hanging around," their father said. "The longer we stay the harder it'll be. Better to make a clean break." Alice thought of the sticks Isaac snapped over his knee to get the fire going in winter, the way they crackled and spit in the flames.

Their mother and Flora checked and double-checked the contents of the trunk; pinafores, shirts, underwear and sweaters were folded, unfolded and folded again until Alice said, "I have everything I need. Can we just go?" and Isaac lifted the trunk into the boot of the car.

Edna, Alice and their mother were ready and waiting by the car as their father came out of the house. Flora stood behind him in the doorway. He hesitated. "On second thought," he said.

"What?" said their mother walking towards him. "What is it?"

Alice thought for a moment he had decided not to send her away.

"I think I should stay at home," he said, "with Edna."

"What are you saying?" their mother said.

"I mean I think it's going to be difficult for the girls to say goodbye. Edna should stay here with me."

"I want to go," said Edna.

Their father knelt beside Alice and held her shoulders. "You don't want to see your sister getting upset do you?"

"It's such a long way," said their mother. "I can't drive all that way and back. I'll stay with Edna."

"No, no, no," their father shook his head. "The child needs her mother, don't you, Alice?" He took a card from his inside pocket. "Here. I've written the name of a guest house near the school. I've booked a room for you. You can drive back in the morning." He held the card out. Their mother stared at it. She stared at their father then slowly took the card. They all stood waiting to see what happened next.

"Come on, Alice, in the car." Their mother climbed into the driver's seat and slammed the door and, before Alice had closed the passenger door, the car's wheels were spinning on the driveway and they were off. Alice blew kisses to Edna from the back window. Flora stayed in the shadows of the porch.

After breakfast Alice and Edna were sitting near their hideout talking about what they should do when something landed on the grass next to them. It was a pine cone. Another one came down, this time hitting Alice on the leg. She stood and went to the hedge. "Katie?" said Alice.

"About time," said a voice on the other side of the hedge. Alice pulled at the branches at the bottom of the hedge until she could see Katie's face. "Where have you been?" said Katie.

"We've been busy," said Alice.

"Doing what?"

"I don't know, helping out," said Alice.

"Why are you whispering?"

"I don't know if I can let you in, Katie."

Every summer Alice and Katie pulled the branches away on either side of the hedge until there was a tunnel between their gardens and every year Isaac patched it over with chicken wire. Katie's garden backed on to theirs, which meant to visit her they would have to be taken into the next street. Their mothers turned a blind eye but Isaac scolded them for damaging the garden.

"Come on," said Katie. "You lift the wire, Alice. Edna, you there?"

"I'm here," said Edna from behind Alice.

"You hold back the thorns," said Katie. "I don't want to tear this stupid dress."

Katie was taller than Alice and lean and strong. She boasted that she could run faster than any boy she knew and liked to wear short trousers and polo shirts but her mother insisted on her wearing summer dresses and tying her hair in pigtails. Alice checked behind to see that no one was watching them and pulled the wire up as high as it would go. Katie scrambled under and stood up, dusting her dress down.

"We're building a new hideout," said Edna.

"I thought you'd have been far too busy for that," said Katie, sitting in the long grass. Edna and Alice sat down beside her.

"We're just starting," said Alice.

"You can help if you like," said Edna.

Katie put a piece of grass between her teeth and shrugged her shoulders. "How's the prison?" she said. Katie went to a day school in the town. The day school was mixed and Alice and Edna never tired of hearing about the trouble the boys got into and about her brothers who once dared Katie to look into the furled leaf of a banana tree while they hit it to flush out the bats.

"Shall we get on with it then?" said Katie.

"With what?" said Alice.

"The new den," said Katie. "What's wrong with you two?"

They looked around for things to build with. At the side of the shed they found an old garden gate that had come off its hinges. "Perfect," said Katie. "It's like a story I read once about villains who steal a door from a house and put it in a tree so they can hide up there whenever the police are out looking."

"But we haven't done anything wrong," said Edna. "Have we?"

"No," said Katie, "but we can pretend."

Katie looked for the right tree then climbed into a pine whose trunk separated into a perfect foothold. Alice and Edna lifted the gate for her to pull up and she balanced it between the branches. "It's great," she shouted down. "We just need sticks to build it up a bit, so we're hidden." She jumped down. They'd seen a pile of cuttings behind the shed and they went and scooped up armfuls of branches. Again, Katie climbed and Alice and Edna passed them up.

"Come on up," she said and Alice made a basket with her hands for Edna to step on, then she climbed up herself.

"This is the best hideout yet," said Edna. They stacked the branches around the edges of the gate, weaving twigs through each other to make it stable, then sat cross-legged wondering what to do.

"I'm parched," said Katie. "How about some of your mother's lemonade?"

"She's not here," said Edna.

"When she gets back then, how long will that be?"

"She's not coming back," said Edna.

"They're dead," said Alice.

"What?"

"Our parents," said Alice, "killed in a car accident."

"They were on holiday," said Edna.

"That's terrible. When?" said Katie.

"We don't know," said Edna, starting to cry.

"So who's looking after you?"

"Magdalena," said Alice. "And Isaac."

"The garden boy?" said Katie. She made a face like she'd tasted something rotten. "He gives me the creeps."

"Katie, we're going," someone shouted from her garden.

"My brother," said Katie. She jumped down. "Quick, lift the wire for me." Alice jumped from the tree and held the wire while Katie slithered under the hedge. "I'll see you tomorrow," she shouted, her voice disappearing down the length of her garden.

Magdalena gave the girls jobs to do. They swept floors, hung up rugs and beat out clouds of dust. They cracked nuts, put them in jars and brushed the shells under the house. Now and again, when Alice remembered what Magdalena had told them, she pushed it out of her mind and when they ate outside that night the dog frightened her less, asleep with its snout resting on its paws.

In bed she told Edna a story about two girls who lived alone in a house they'd built themselves out of odds and ends swept up on the beach. Edna joined in until they had a fabulous windswept palace where they went barefoot and ate with their hands but, once Edna was asleep, Alice saw the waves that grew in the night. They rolled in closer and closer until they swallowed the palace up. Everything they had tied and fastened together came undone and floated out to sea with Alice and Edna clinging on, waiting to be rescued.

Alice felt cold and tried to reach for the blankets but

someone was pulling them away from her. "Get up now, Alice. We have to go." It was Magdalena. "Hurry please. Wake your sister and come downstairs."

Alice looked behind the curtain. The night was pitch black. She crawled to the end of the bed and shook Edna's shoulder. She didn't flinch. Alice shook her harder.

"Leave me alone," mumbled Edna.

"You have to wake up."

"Is it morning?"

"No," said Alice, "not yet."

Edna pulled the covers over her head but Alice pulled them down.

"We have to get dressed," said Alice. "Come on, I'll help you."

She turned the bedside light on and took clothes from their drawers. She helped Edna find her sleeves and wriggle her feet into her socks. It was cold and she found their winter sweaters at the back of the cupboard and gave one to Edna.

"It scratches," said Edna.

"It's better than freezing," said Alice.

"Where are we going?" said Edna.

"I don't know."

Magdalena was waiting for them at the bottom of the stairs. She was wearing an overcoat and carrying a handbag. "Hurry," she said. She locked the front door and put the key in her bag. They ran down the driveway to keep up with her until she stopped at the gate. She looked up and down the road but it was empty. "We need a taxi," she said. Alice knew that what she meant by a taxi was a minibus crammed as full as it could possibly be. Her father always overtook them pushing them into the side of the road.

"We'll have to go to the main road," said Magdalena and they walked along the grass verge past the high walls of the neighbours' gardens. Alice wondered what they would say if they looked out of their windows and saw her and Edna out with the maid in the middle of the night. But the street was badly lit and, wrapped up as they were, they would easily be mistaken for black children and not given a second thought.

At the intersection a car passed every so often, its lights bouncing as it hit the potholes. Magdalena stepped into the road and waved her arm. The taxi was full of people on their way home, their heads leaned against the windows with their eyes shut or their heads nodding when they couldn't stay awake. Magdalena squeezed herself between the seats and they stood in the aisle. She held on to the luggage rack, Alice held on to her and Edna held on to Alice.

"It's not far," whispered Magdalena.

It was far, and by the time they came to their stop they were the only ones left in the taxi. It was dark and they followed Magdalena along a narrow path that wound through houses propped up against each other. Some had walls built from brick, others were sheets of corrugated iron patched with lengths of sackcloth. Edna held her nose but Alice slapped her hand away and made a face that told Edna she shouldn't do it again, but the smell was nastier than anything she'd ever smelt. Men and women stood in their doorways and spoke to Magdalena as they passed, looked at the girls then spoke again. Some of them laughed. Alice took Edna's hand. The path opened out on to a square and Magdalena stopped in front of a building that looked more like a house than the others around it. "We are here," she said.

Inside it was darker still and Alice couldn't make out a thing. She squeezed Edna's hand. Magdalena pulled back a curtain and they ducked under her arm into a second room. A bare light bulb lit the room and in the corner stood a woman who, even from behind, Edna recognised.

"Flora," said Edna. She let go of Alice's hand and ran to her then stopped. A boy lay in the bed, his body hardly making a bump under the blankets. Flora lifted the cloth from his forehead, dipped it in the basin at her feet, wrung it out and placed it back where it was. The boy's eyes were closed but he flinched as the cool water met his skin.

"The boy is very sick," said Flora. Magdalena took Edna by the shoulders and led her and Alice back into the first room. She hooked the curtain up so the light spilled into the room. There were two beds pushed up against the wall with thin mattresses on them that drooped in the middle like hammocks and Magdalena pointed at the furthest one.

"Sit there for now," she said.

The girls perched next to each other on the edge of the bed. "What's wrong with him?" said Edna.

"We don't know," said Magdalena.

"Is he your son?" said Alice.

"My nephew," said Magdalena. She took a blanket from the other bed, wrapped it round their shoulders and left them alone. The girls huddled together and listened to the mumblings from the next room. Flora's voice grew louder. She was angry but Magdalena came back at her and then they fell quiet.

"What are they fighting about?" whispered Edna.

"I don't know," said Alice.

"If he's her nephew," said Alice, "that means Flora is her sister. And sisters argue sometimes, like us, but it doesn't mean anything."

It fell quiet in the next room and they heard the noise of dishes and pans. Soon a strong smell of fish filled the air. Magdalena came in with two plates and handed them to the girls.

"Eat this," she said, "then get some sleep."

Alice looked down at the slop of little fish on the green plastic plate. She tipped it and they slid to the other side.

"I don't think I can eat it," said Edna.

"We have to," said Alice, taking the spoon and lifting the smallest mouthful to her lips. The smell was so strong her stomach clenched. "Eat them whole," she said. She shut her eyes and ate. She was hungry and the taste was better than the smell. She ate some more. Edna watched her and ate as well. When their plates were clean Alice stacked them and put them on the floor next to the bed.

When Alice woke there was a row of faces at the window. She sat up and the children giggled and ran away. She shook Edna's shoulder but she only squirmed under the blanket. From the other room Alice heard crying. She sat very still. The crying came in waves. Loud sobs calmed into shallow gasps then grew again. Where there two people crying or one? It was hard to tell. Then she heard Magdalena's voice. It was low and pleading and as she spoke the crying shrunk to a moan then the room went quiet until the calm broke. The sobs came in a torrent this time. Magdalena came into the room and stood by the side of the bed the girls lay on.

"The boy was too ill," she said. "He stopped breathing."

Alice felt Edna's hot breath on her arm. She looked at Magdalena's bloodshot eyes.

"We will wait," she said, "and bury him this afternoon." Then she shuffled back to the other room stooped over like an old woman.

"Has she gone?" said Edna from under the blankets.

"She's gone," Alice said and slid under the blankets too. They lay on their backs keeping quiet. The light shone through the coarse weave like stars on a night sky.

"What will we do now?" said Edna.

"We will be brave," said Alice. "We'll do what we're told and we'll be brave."

Magdalena showed them where they could pee and gave them a bowl of meal each and they sat on the bed with the blanket pulled over their knees and watched the quiet stream of people that came in and out of the house. The first was a minister clutching a cross in his hand and they listened to the thrum of his voice as he read passages from the Bible. Flora was quiet. Alice pictured her holding the boy's hand and nodding to the minister's words. When he left, friends and neighbours came to pay their respects. Women brought their children and while they wept with Flora the boys and girls peered into the room where Alice and Edna sat on the bed.

When the flow of visitors stopped Magdalena came to them.

"We will take him now," she said.

Behind her stood two men. One held a bundle in his arms and the other supported Flora. She stumbled and Magdalena went to the other side of her and held her arm.

"Walk behind us," said Magdalena.

Alice and Edna climbed off the bed and followed them out of the house. It was bright and warm outside and for a moment Alice felt relieved to be out of that room. As they walked through the houses people joined them. The narrow streets became congested. Alice held Edna's hand and kept Magdalena's red sweater in sight. The procession started singing, first in a low hum then in full, clear voices until, when they came to a patch of wasteland at the edge of the buildings, the crowd was singing and stamping their feet as they walked.

They followed a track across a field littered with scrap metal and discarded furniture until they came to a gate that opened into a graveyard of simple wooden crosses and the occasional headstone. A hole had already been dug and the minister that had been in the house that morning stood, Bible open, by a mound of earth.

The girls hung back but Magdalena took them by the hand and brought them into the circle that had formed round the hole in the ground and held them close. Flora knelt by the freshly dug earth sobbing and shaking while everyone sang and two of the men lowered the body into the grave.

Magdalena held their hands tighter and Alice was glad because she felt her legs wobble and thought they might give way under her. Had their parents been buried already? Had they been put in the ground where they died, there and then, or would their bodies be brought back to the house? She wanted to go home, to be there in case someone came to call. Maybe no one had heard yet but they should be there. Maybe their grandparents were travelling now, driving across the country to take them back to their home. Her hand was hurting now. Magdalena was squeezing it so tightly but she was glad. She was glad of the distraction and the certainty of the pain.

When the crowd had turned back to their houses and the men had patted the last of the soil down with their spades they lifted Flora from the ground and draped her arms around their shoulders and walked her away from the grave. Alice took a last look at the fresh patch of earth and followed Magdalena and Edna until they reached the house.

"Wait here," she said to them when they got to the front door. She went into the house and came out seconds later.

"I'll take you home," she said.

They walked back to the main road and waited for a minibus. The sky was pink and night was coming. Magdalena flagged a bus down. It wasn't as crowded as the previous day and they took their seats. Edna fell asleep with her head on Magdalena's knee.

The driver stopped outside their gate and as they walked up the driveway Alice saw flames licking the sky behind the pines. Through the silhouetted trees she could see Isaac breaking branches and throwing them on the fire. Sparks rose and swirled around and above him.

"The hideout," said Edna. "He's burning the hideout."

"Come," said Magdalena, "it will be better tomorrow."

The next morning Alice lay on her stomach under the hedge watching for Katie to pass. Finally she stuck her head under the wire. Katie's brother Garth ran over.

"What do you want?" he said.

"Is Katie there?" said Alice.

"She's in the house," said Garth. He stood looking down at Alice.

"Can you get her?"

Garth stomped up the garden banging his tennis racquet against his calf. Alice backed through the hedge and sat beside Edna who was threading grass through the pattern of holes in her shoe.

"He's gone to get her," said Alice.

They waited until they could see Katie's plimsolls through the leaves.

"Come through," said Alice.

"I'm not allowed," said Katie.

"Why not?" said Alice.

"My mother says you make up unkind stories. I'm not to talk to you any more."

"What stories?"

"About your parents. My mother says it's cruel to lie about death."

"They're not stories." Alice thought about the boy in the bed, the taxi ride and the crying round the grave. "They're not stories," she said again.

"Your parents are on holiday." They heard her footsteps fade as she ran away from the hedge, then she shouted back, "My mother said so!"

Edna looked at Alice.

"Come on," said Alice. "Let's go inside."

The walls of their parents' bedroom were covered in wallpaper patterned with brown and gold flowers and they ran their hands over the raised velvet. Their mother's dressing table was shaped like a kidney and the stool that tucked into the curve was wide enough for them both to sit on. Fabric hung from its glass top to the floor, making it a perfect hiding place.

"Shall we dress up?" said Edna. Alice went on brushing her hair. "No, I don't feel like it either." It was their favourite thing to do when their mother was out and it was too hot to play outside or when it rained, but it didn't feel right today. Alice pulled the fabric to one side and opened the drawer. Objects were arranged in neat piles: a silk scarf, a lipstick, a satin purse and a wristwatch that no longer worked. They touched each thing one by one with their fingertips, then Alice closed the drawer but it jammed. "Something's stuck," she said and pulled it back out, crouched down and ran her hand behind it. Something fell to the floor and Edna crawled behind the fabric and pulled out a long rectangular box.

"The bracelet," said Alice.

She'd recognised immediately the embossed leather that felt and looked like snakeskin. Had Flora taken only the bracelet and left the box? She grabbed it from Edna and opened it. The lid sprung open and lying on the dark blue velvet was the tiger's eye bracelet.

"Do you know what this means?" said Alice. Edna shook her head. "It means Flora didn't steal the bracelet. Mother made a mistake."

"Will Flora come back?"

"I don't know," said Alice. "Let's go and show Magdalena."

"What if she's angry?"

"She won't be," said Alice. "It proves Flora didn't do it." Alice shut the box and put it in her pocket. "Come on."

Edna walked behind Alice, down the hallway and down the stairs. Alice was in a hurry and Edna ran a little to keep up. Alice looked for Magdalena in one room after the other. Each one was empty.

"She must be in the back," said Alice and she started down the hall to the kitchen.

"Wait for me," said Edna.

The kitchen was empty and the back door open.

"Magdalena!" Alice shouted. There was no answer. "Maybe she's taking a nap."

"The dog," said Edna stopping at the door.

"It's tied up," said Alice.

The dog snarled and hunkered to the ground. Alice kicked a dry bone towards it and it growled. The girls ran past it. They didn't play round the back of the house but at the same time they'd never been told it was off limits. Alice pushed the door and it swung ajar. It was dark inside. They heard a grunt like the noises Magdalena made when she was sleeping. They heard it again. Edna looked past Alice and saw something move. She saw Isaac with his trousers at his feet and the gleam of sweat on his clenched buttocks. She saw Magdalena bent over the table, her apron pulled up round her waist and her huge knickers on the floor.

Alice grabbed Edna's hand and they ran. They ran round to the front of the house, scratching their legs on the bushes they jumped through. They ran across the lawn, leapt over the borders and nearly crashed into the post boy, who skidded his bike to a standstill.

"What's the rush?" he laughed.

Alice and Edna panted and bent over to catch their breath. The post boy opened his satchel and took out a bundle of brown envelopes and from between them he pulled a postcard. He handed it to Edna.

"This one's for you," he said.

Edna looked at the words "table" and "mountain" printed diagonally across the photograph in curly red writing. Alice came up behind her.

"What is it?"

Edna held up the postcard for her to see. Her mother's handwriting was big and a few lines filled the space but it was joined up and hard to read. She handed it to Alice.

"She wrote it on Monday, before the accident," said Alice

"How do you know?"

She turned the card over and pointed to the top right-hand corner. "Look, it says Monday and the date, and that has to be before the accident because she couldn't write it after the accident, could she?" She turned it back over and they looked at the picture.

"I'll take that." Magdalena reached over Alice's shoulder and took the postcard. She put it in her apron pocket. The post boy tipped his hat and rode away.

"You dropped this," said Magdalena holding out the mock snakeskin jewellery case. Alice patted her pocket. She hadn't noticed it falling out.

"We were coming to show you," started Alice.

"I want you to put it back."

"But Flora didn't take it."

"Put it back," said Magdalena, "exactly where you found it."

"But it had fallen down the back of the dressing table. The drawer was jammed," said Alice. Her eyes were filling with tears.

"Exactly," said Magdalena, putting the case in Alice's hand, "where you found it."

Alice opened the drawer, slid her hand behind it, wedged the jewellery case into the space and closed the drawer quickly to stop it falling. She turned the small key in the wardrobe door and pushed the clothes to one side. Edna climbed in and Alice followed her. They wriggled into the spaces between the shoes and Alice pulled the door behind her until it was only open a finger's width. They breathed in the musty smell of mothballs and fur.

"Why didn't they take us, Alice?"

"On holiday? Grown-ups need time alone, Edna," said Alice. "At least that's what Mummy always says," she said quietly.

They sat for a while waiting for sounds from downstairs but nothing came. Edna hummed a nursery rhyme then she fell quiet.

"Flora's better at kissing than mother," she said.

"What are you talking about?" said Alice, rearranging herself to face Edna.

"She's better at kissing."

"I heard you. When has Flora ever kissed you?"

"She's kissed Daddy and he likes her kisses more than Mummy's kisses."

"Do you know what you're saying?" said Alice. "When did she kiss Daddy?"

"When you went away to school," said Edna. "She kissed him on the lips."

The night their mother had taken Alice to school Flora sat with Edna and her father at the dinner table. It was her father who set the extra place. He took the best cutlery from the chest and put it next to his setting. Flora didn't want to sit down but Edna saw her smile behind her hand and when their father pulled the chair out she giggled and let him push her in. They passed the dishes of mashed potatoes and peas between them. Edna took more than usual and nobody noticed. Their father forked slices of chicken on to their plates and passed the gravy boat around. He poured wine into his own glass then a little into Flora's.

Edna couldn't sleep that night. She was lonely without Alice and the bedroom felt too large and dark. She tiptoed downstairs and along the hall to their father's study. She could see the light was still on and she pushed open the door. On the other side of the desk their father leaned back in his chair with his eyes shut. His mouth was open and a sound was coming out of him in huffs and sighs. She stood for a while watching him twitch like a dog in a dream.

"Jesus, Edna," he said suddenly and rummaged behind his desk. He pushed something away and Flora stood up. She stood to one side next to the bookshelves but didn't leave the room. Edna went round to her father. He smelt of whisky. An unlit cigar lay on his desk next to an open book. On the facing page was a template of a kingfisher.

"I rescued one of those," said Edna pointing to the picture.

Her father laughed too loudly. He looked across at Flora and smoothed down his hair. "Was this a game you played with Alice?"

"No," said Edna. "I found it on the ground. Isaac helped me look after it."

"It was making a nest most likely," said her father. "They slam into the ground to make an opening for a tunnel."

"Doesn't it hurt?"

"Sometimes it kills them."

"But why do they do it then?" said Edna.

"It's how they make their home," he said. "It's what they've always done, Edna. Birds don't think like we do." He closed the book and pushed her towards the door. "Back upstairs now, Edna. And straight to bed."

By the time Alice finished her first year at boarding school Flora's belly was large and round. She crouched down to pick things up because she couldn't bend forwards and Alice saw her rubbing the small of her back as she stood at the sink. Then one day she went away. Alice remembered because their mother cooked the dinner and she remembered their father pushing away the plate of burnt meat that she had tried to cover over with lumpy gravy. But Flora was back the next day. She was changing the beds upstairs when Alice found her clutching a towel to her chest. Her blouse was soaked through.

"Where is your baby?" Alice remembered asking.

"My sister is looking after him."

"Why don't you look after him?"

Flora rubbed at her chest and hung the towel on the rail.

"I have you two to look after," she said shaking a sheet over the bed. "And this house."

They must have fallen asleep in the wardrobe because when Alice woke she struggled to remember where she was and tried to straighten out her legs. The door burst open. She carried Edna from the wardrobe and lay her on her bed. Plates of crackers and glasses of milk had been left on their bedside cabinets. Edna stirred.

"Tomorrow we could run away," she said then fell asleep again.

When Alice woke up in the morning, Edna's bed was empty. Alice ran to look out the window and saw her crouched at the side of the driveway. It had rained in the night, leaving small puddles that would dry up as the day went on. Edna was placing twigs in the open leaves of the Venus flytraps that ran the length of the borders. She'd been told not to do that. "It teases them," their father said. "They think they're going to eat and they can't open their leaves again so they die." After that Edna found flies to feed them. She collected handfuls from the windowsills around the house and placed them one by one into the mouths of the plants and watched their teeth close around them. But Alice could see Edna picking up twigs, breaking stems to find anything at all to close the plants. She should go out and tell her off, tell her she'd help her find flies. They could do it together. Alice picked at a piece of loose paint next to the glass then Edna started to run.

The car swung through the gates flashing its headlights and the sun glinted off the metallic blue bonnet. Their mother leaned out of the window waving her arm, her pearl bracelet slipping up her forearm. "We've got presents," she shouted. Edna chased behind the car as their father pulled up in front of the house and threw her arms round their mother's waist before she was fully upright. She laughed and patted Edna on the back. "I've missed you too, darling," she said. Alice ran down the stairs, past Magdalena, and out of the front door, letting it swing wide open behind her.

Heartfelt thanks to Elizabeth Reeder for her encouragement and energy, to Zoe Strachan for her valuable guidance, to Allan Cameron and Dana Keller at Vagabond Voices for everything that has brought this book into existence, to Mark Mechan for a beautiful cover, and to all my friends who have read and listened and advised me – Duncan Muir for his sharp edits, Tatiana Lund for her travelling negatives, Rosie Hopkins and Walt Hopkins for their constant and generous support – and to Stuart, Lily, Blu and Eric: the whirlwind that is my family.

An extract from "The Nest" was published in *The Flight of the Turtle: New Writing Scotland 29*.